PARKER'S COLT

A Novel of New Mexico Ranch Life

PARKER'S COLT

A Novel of New Mexico Ranch Life

Stephen Zimmer

SUNSTONE
PRESS

SANTA FE

Sunstone books may be purchased for educational, business, or sales promotional use.
For information please write: Special Markets Department, Sunstone Press,
P.O. Box 2321, Santa Fe, New Mexico 87504-2321.

Book and Cover design ▷ Vicki Ahl
Body typeface ▷ Americana
Printed on acid free paper

Library of Congress Cataloging-in-Publication Data

Zimmer, Stephen.
   Parker's colt : a novel of New Mexico ranch life / by Stephen Zimmer.
      p. cm.
   ISBN 978-0-86534-810-3 (softcovers : alk. paper)
   1. Ranch life–New Mexico–Fiction. 2. Teenage boys–Fiction. 3. Horses--Fiction.
4. Human-animal relationships–Fiction. I. Title.
   PS3626.I4885P37 2011
   813'.6--dc22

                                          2011017267

WWW.SUNSTONEPRESS.COM
SUNSTONE PRESS / POST OFFICE BOX 2321 / SANTA FE, NM 87504-2321 /USA
(505) 988-4418 / ORDERS ONLY (800) 243-5644 / FAX (505) 988-1025

1

THE NEW COLT

The colt was standing with its mother on the far side of the pasture. Parker Smith slowly walked up, hardly able to contain himself because he was so anxious to find out whether it was a filly or a horse colt. The New Mexico sun had just come up in the east on his parents' ranch, the Box S, and caused the mountains in the west to glow purple and red.

The mare turned her head, gave him an unconcerned look, and returned to eating the grass at her feet. Parker walked to her right side to look at the colt, and when he was close enough, knelt down and peered underneath. He had told his dad he didn't care what it turned out to be, but to himself, he hoped it would be a horse colt.

A smile came to his face when he saw that it was. He could hardly keep from running up to it and rubbing its neck, but knew that he would just scare it. Instead, he did the next best thing and took off at a high lope to go tell his mother and father.

He found his mother, Ann, in the kitchen cooking breakfast. He ran and hugged her, sputtering that he had a horse colt. She smiled and told him to go tell his dad who was down at the barn. Parker broke from his mother's arms and sprinted out the backdoor.

He ran so fast that he almost smashed into the corral gate. As he gathered himself up he saw his dad coming from the saddle house door. Tom Smith was dressed as usual in a white shirt, black boots, and a black hat. His black mustache showed a few tints of grey.

"Dad, I got a horse colt!" he cried as he ran to hug his dad.

"That's great son, I'm glad for you. I knew that's what you really wanted," his dad said as he hugged the boy.

"What are you going to name him?"

"Well, I don't know. I haven't even thought about it," Parker replied.

"All I can say is pick a name that'll fit him because you're going to have him for a long time."

"You bet," said Parker. "Let's go look at him. He's a sorrel just like I wanted and has a bald face and a left hind stocking like his mother. I bet he's going to be plenty cowy."

"That might be, but you know that color doesn't really mean much," his dad said as they walked out the corral gate.

It took them a while to walk through the pasture to get to the mare and colt. When they were about fifty feet away, Parker looked at his Dad to see his reaction.

"Well, there's nothing wrong with how he's made," his Dad said. "Go get a halter and catch Penny and lead 'em into the big pen. You might as well start working with him."

Within an hour, Parker had the mare and colt at the corrals. He gave Penny some grain in a feed bag, and she stood in the middle of the pen while she ate.

The colt explored the new place but made sure he stayed closer to his mother than the boy. Parker stood by the fence with his arms folded and admired the little horse. He felt lucky and proud at the same time and couldn't wait to start working with him. But he knew he'd have to bide his time and not do anything too quick that might scare the colt.

After Penny finished her oats, she walked up to Parker to let him pull off the feed bag. Parker stroked her neck and scratched her behind the ears. She cocked her head to help guide him to get the greatest benefit from his fingers.

While Parker was standing by the mare, the colt walked up on the offside and started nudging his mother's udder in order to get a drink. Parker stroked down the mare's withers and back, and as he did, he bent down to watch the colt suck. He moved his right hand down the mare's flank as close to the colt's head as he dared, hoping that the colt would get a whiff of his smell mixed with his mother's. He knew that getting the colt used to his smell would help gentle him.

He stood a while longer and after a final pat on the mare's neck, he walked to the corral gate. The mare followed him with the colt behind. He pushed the gate open and stepped aside so the horses could go back to the pasture.

The colt kicked up his heels as he followed his mother who broke into a trot toward her favorite spot by the river. Parker smiled as he watched and admired the colt's rust colored coat as it glistened in the morning sun.

Then, the colt's name came to him. "I'm going to call him, Rusty," he exclaimed.

The next morning Parker opened his eyes when the sun's first rays came into his east window. He quickly pulled on his shirt and stuck his pants' legs into his red topped boots. He walked to the kitchen that was filled with his favorite smell, frying bacon. His mother smiled at him as she cut out biscuits on the kitchen counter. Without stopping to talk as he usually did, he ran out the back door to go look at his colt.

When he opened the yard gate, he looked up and saw Penny walking toward the water tank for her morning drink without the colt at her side. In a panic, Parker started to call his mother, but in the next second, he saw a reddish blur coming out of the brush by the river. It was Rusty. He had gotten separated from his mother and was doing his best to catch up with her as fast as he could.

"Boy, that little horse's got some jets," Parker said to himself.

Like the morning before, he had to resist the urge to run up to the colt and pet him. While he watched the colt nurse, his mother called out to him to come eat breakfast. He said he'd be just a second and then opened the corral gate to let in the mare and colt.

At breakfast he ate as slowly and politely as he could. At the same time he avoided his parent's eyes, knowing that they would comment on his table manners if he ate too quickly. His parents exchanged smiles several times as they saw how badly their son wanted to get with the colt.

Parker took his last bite of scrambled egg and washed it down with milk. In spite of himself, he squirmed in his seat as he watched his parents finish their breakfast. He thought he was about to be able to go when his Dad reached for another biscuit. It seemed like it took forever for his dad to get the biscuit buttered and to smear on some strawberry jam.

Right before his Dad took a bite though, he said to Parker, "Son, don't you think you ought to get that mare fed?"

Although his dad's question caught him by surprise, Parker grinned and said, "Yes sir! Come out and look at Rusty when you can."

After he grained the mare, he stroked her back on the side where the colt had begun to nurse. The colt was less wary than he'd been the day before and after about thirty minutes, he began to investigate the boy's hand with his nose.

Parker let the colt smell his hand. Rusty wrinkled his nose at the scent, but sniffed again and decided it wasn't so bad. It was as if he said to himself that if his mom didn't mind the two-legged boy touching her, it couldn't be so bad for him either.

When Parker turned the mare and colt out of the gate and they headed for the pasture, he admitted to himself that it was a pretty darn good colt.

2

CROSS L GATHER

At 4:30 the next morning, Tom Smith walked down the hall and into his son's room to wake him up.

"Roll out, compadre. Your mother almost has breakfast," he said.

Parker pushed down the covers, sat up, and reached for his shirt.

"By gosh, I wish you'd get up that quick when you go to school," his dad said.

"Well, if school was as much fun as branding, I bet I would," Parker said smiling at his dad. He finished dressing as quick as he could and pulled on his boots and spurs. "I hope mom doesn't say anything about my spurs being on my boots," he said to himself.

When he walked into the kitchen, his mother quickly looked at him and said with a smile, "You sure you need those spurs to eat breakfast, cowboy?"

"Oh, Mom, you know I'm just going to go out and get horseback in a minute anyway," Parker said.

"Yes, I know, but I also know how rowels put marks on my chairs. Even your father does it," she replied. "We need to get back to the rule that you guys leave 'em on the back porch."

"Okay," he said, but in a way that said it was a rule he didn't agree with. But, he figured she wouldn't appreciate that his idol, Donnie Jeffers, had told him that real cowpunchers never took their spurs off their boots.

Parker sat at the table and ate his bacon and eggs without much conversation. He was too excited. The branding was at the Cross Ls, and even though he knew they'd have a lot of help, he hoped that he'd get to drag some calves.

When he got up to take his plate to the sink, his dad walked in the back door from feeding the horses. Parker turned to him and asked, "You reckon they'll let me drag any today?"

"I bet so, especially considering how many calves you've flanked for 'em the last two years," his Dad replied.

Parker walked to the back door, grabbed his hat, and stepped outside. As usual, his black and white border collie, Josie, was waiting for him. He scratched her ears and as he walked out the gate, she trailed after him. There was barely any color showing on the eastern horizon, and even though he couldn't see very well, he still ran to the corrals and turned on the light in the saddle house.

After he saddled his horse, Chester, he led him to the trailer and loaded him. Chester was eight years old and the son of Penny's half sister. As the cowboys say, he was a well-made dun with a dark line down his back. He was stocky and not too tall and had the kind of disposition cowboys like. He was gentle and only bucked when he was feeling good on early mornings in the spring. It seemed that everybody commented about how obvious it was that Chester liked Parker. Every time Parker walked into the horse trap, Chester nickered at him and trotted over to get his ears scratched and get a piece of horse cake.

His dad soon came with his horse. Once they closed the

trailer gate, Parker started to get in on the passenger side.

As he reached to open the door, his dad asked, "Don't you want to drive?"

"You mean you'd let me. I thought I couldn't drive on the highway."

"Oh, let's don't worry about it. I doubt there's going to be any state troopers around at this time of the morning. Go ahead, go on and get in."

Parker was so excited he almost tripped over his spurs. He went around to the driver's side and jumped in. After he adjusted the seat, he started the truck, put it in gear, and slowly started toward the cattle guard. He looked at the house and saw his mother watching. He gave her a big smile and a wave as he drove past.

It was a twenty-five mile drive to the Cross Ls, which meant it was the farthest Parker had ever driven on a highway. They got to the headquarters about 6:00 o'clock, and Parker drove the trailer to the west side of the corrals. There were two other trucks and trailers already there, his best friend, Joe Dan Peters and his dad, and a cowboy from the Swenson Ranch named Curtis Ford. They had already unloaded their horses and were walking toward the main gate.

Parker parked the truck, and he and his dad unloaded their horses. After they mounted, they trotted to catch up with the other men. The Cross Ls was the biggest ranch in this part of New Mexico and was owned by a wealthy family back in Connecticut. The owners hardly ever visited except for a week or so in the summer and sometimes at shipping time. Tom Smith once told Parker that he figured that they liked making money off the ranch, but they didn't want to have to live there. Probably too uncivilized for them, and besides, the wind blew too hard.

When they got to the big corral, Parker rode up beside Joe Dan and they shook hands. "How'd you beat us here?" Parker said. "I thought you never got up before ten."

"Oh, big talker, you know I generally have a day's work done before you even think about getting out of that crib of yours," Joe Dan replied, grinning at his friend.

Joe Dan and Parker had been best friends since they'd met five years ago midway through third grade when Joe Dan's parents bought the ranch headquartered at the mouth of Highland Canyon that was southwest of Parker's. Joe Dan was the same age as Parker, but shorter, and had brown hair that always hung in his face when he didn't have his hat on. There were two other important things about him, first, you could always count on him having a smile on his face, and, second, you could always count on him to be talking. It never bothered Parker though, because he loved to hear whatever he said just to hear the way he said it.

John Robles, the cow boss of the Cross Ls, rode up to the boys and said, "We appreciate you boys coming. If you don't mind, go with James and Curtis and take the outside circle. That'll give your dads and me time to get a fire started and get the irons hot."

The boys said that'd be fine and they rode across the corral at a trot to the other side where James and Curtis were waiting at the outside gate. When they got there, they said hello and shook hands with the older cowboys. James was off his horse to open the gate, and when everyone had ridden through, he said, "Boys, there ain't no better time in the world than when we get to smell that burnin' hair."

Everyone nodded in agreement. Branding in the spring was easily the favorite time of the year for everybody. The ranchers got to see the increase of their herds and put their ownership mark on them, whereas the cowboys got to see a lot of friends they sometimes hadn't seen for an entire year.

The boys were glad that they had been sent with James and Curtis. Along with Donnie, they were the boys' favorites and it was always fun to get to ride with them. They were both good hands and could ride bucking horses and rope as well as anybody in the country. They were also pretty entertaining, always pulling pranks, telling jokes or saying ordinary things in unusual ways.

Curtis had been raised on his dad's little hay farm over by Springer. Even though his dad had a nice herd of cows, Curtis wanted to ride on the big ranches and see as much country as he could from the back of a horse. He had said several times that he knew that someday he'd go back home and help his dad, but in the meantime, he was going to be a big outfit cowboy. Even though he was only twenty-five, he'd already spent a lot of time on the big IL Ranch in Nevada and the Pitchforks in Wyoming. He was back in the county because his mother had been sick, and he wanted to be closer to her while she got better. Still he was doing what he wanted to do because the Swensons had over 300,000 acres and ran more than 4,500 mother cows.

James Baird, on the other hand, was from Georgia and had come to New Mexico when he was eighteen to work at a dude ranch. Soon after he arrived, he discovered that he'd rather punch cows and do real work instead of herding dudes. In the six years since he'd been riding for the Cross Ls, he'd become a top hand, so good in fact that John had installed him as his *segundo*, the second man in charge.

James closed the gate, stepped back on his horse, and led the riders at a lope to the far end of the pasture. Once there, he asked Curtis if he wouldn't mind taking Parker with him and ride the outside circle.

"I'll take Joe Dan with me, and we'll see if there's anything in those two draws," he said, pointing to the west.

He reined in that direction and Joe Dan fell in beside him.

"What'd ya call that bronco?" James asked as they trotted along.

"Centavo," Joe Dan said with a smile.

"He sure is well made. How old is he?" James asked.

"Almost as old as I am," Joe Dan replied. "My dad broke him, and we've been pretty good partners ever since he gave him to me a couple of years ago."

"Do ya drag off of him?"

"You bet. He can drag everything I can catch. Problem is, he gets a little upset with me whenever I miss."

"I know what you're talking about. I miss a few my own self once in a while."

They started up the first draw that led down from Gonzalitos Mesa to their left. Two cows with their calves peered at them from behind a big juniper but were unable to stand the pressure of the cowboys looking at them, so they started trotting off to hide further in the brush.

"You'd think these cattle had never seen a horse and a rider before," James said as he spurred his horse to cut them off. Joe Dan went with him, and they were soon behind the cows and had them headed down the draw.

"Joe Dan, would you mind riding out the rest of this? I'd better stay behind these girls in case they start trying to hide again."

"Sure," Joe Dan said. It pleased him that James trusted him enough to send him by himself. He kicked Centavo into a trot and was soon seeing quite of few pairs as he traveled along.

When he got to the head of the draw, he rode all the way to the barbed wire fence that kept the cattle from going farther up the side of the mesa and looked on the other side to see if he could see any tracks. Satisfied that nothing had slipped across, he turned and started down the draw, picking up pairs as he rode along.

He counted twenty-three pairs in his bunch when he got to the bottom. As he eased them around a big rock outcrop, he saw James sitting on his horse with his two pair. Trying to not grin too much, he said, "James, this is all that I could find."

"I never would have thought there would have been that many up there. Good work, cowboy," James said.

Once Joe Dan's cows had mixed with James', the cowboys pointed them toward the corrals that set in the middle of the pasture two miles away. On their right they saw Curtis and Parker coming with about fifty head, and closer to the corrals but on the other side, they saw the dust of the biggest bunch of cattle that were being brought in by John Robles, Tom Smith, and the others.

It took James and Joe Dan almost an hour to get their cattle to the corrals. They threw in with Curtis and Parker when they got to them, and together they picked up another thirty-five pairs as they trailed along.

When they were almost to the corrals, James rode up the right side of the herd and started easing the leaders into the gate, while Curtis did the same on the other side. Parker and Joe Dan stayed in the drags doing their best to keep the calves close to their mothers.

"Don't push 'em too hard, boys," James yelled to them. "I'd hate it if one of 'em cut back on you," he said with a grin.

The boys smiled at each other. They knew that that was exactly what James wanted to happen so that he could rope it.

Once most of the cattle were in the corral James and Curtis dropped back to help Parker and Joe Dan. Unfortunately for James and his chance for roping, they got all of the cattle through the gate without any calves cutting back.

Curtis stepped off his horse to close the gate. As he did, they heard a commotion and yelling from across the other side of the corral where John and his crew were penning their cattle. They hadn't been as fortunate to get all of their calves in. Three had cut back and were heading back into the pasture at a fast run.

James saw John motion to him to come help. "Come on Curtis. Them boys seem to have had a little bad luck. I guess we're gonna have to help 'em out," he said with a grin.

They loped to the other side of the corral and without waiting for instructions, they pulled their ropes from their saddle horns and each took after a calf. Curtis got to his first and threw a nice loop around its neck. After he pulled his slack, he reined in his horse and slowed as easy as he could so as not to jerk the calf too hard. When he got the calf stopped, he stepped off and walked down the rope, pulling a pigging string from his leggings as he went. He grabbed the calf on its right side, and flanked it to the ground. After he had it tied, he took the loop off of its neck and stood up to see what James was doing.

James had missed his calf with his first loop and was still running after him trying to catch him with another loop. As Curtis watched, he said to himself, "Well, there's no better time than the present. I guess I'm gonna have to show the boy how to get his work done." He coiled up his rope, stepped on his horse and took after the third calf. He saw it stopped three hundred yards away. It had turned around and was bawling for its mother.

Curtis slowly eased his horse around it and with a little urging got it moving toward the corrals. After a bit the calf started to trot and then run toward the gate. Curtis followed behind until it was safely through and then turned to see about James.

James had caught his calf in the meantime. Because it was so little, he had picked it up after he roped it and was carrying it with him in the saddle. Curtis trotted up to him and with a smile said, "I thought you were gonna need help, amigo. How many misses does that rope have in it?"

"Don't you worry about it, big guy. I'd rather be good than lucky like you. Besides, I was just trainin' on my horse," James replied with a laugh. He dropped the calf off at the corrals, and then he and Curtis rode back to get the one that Curtis roped. By the time they returned, John and Parker's dad had the branding fire going and had run in some cows and calves into the branding pen.

3

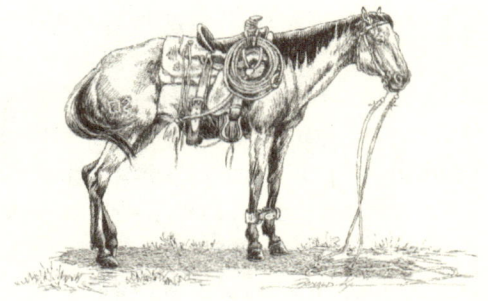

CROSS L BRANDING

"Catch your horse, Chuck," John said to the man who was talking to Tom Smith next to the fence. Parker didn't know Chuck very well because he had been in the country for only about a year since he bought the old Phillips place west of town. He and his wife had fixed it up, and he'd stocked it with a hundred head of cows. Parker's dad told him that Chuck had been a banker for twenty years, but had decided he'd had enough of city life. He'd grown up on a ranch in Arizona, but had moved away when he went to college and was now ready to get back to punching cows.

Chuck was a short man, although strongly built, and walked with a limp. Tom said it had come from getting bucked off a horse when he was a kid. Nevertheless, he always had a smile on his face and liked to give everybody he saw a piece of hard candy from the supply he carried in his pockets, whether they wanted it or not.

He finished talking to Tom and then walked over to his hobbled horse. After checking his cinch and stepping on, he pulled the rope from his saddle, tied a figure-eight knot in the end and pulled it tight over the horn. When he rode into the branding pen, John called out, "Chuck, the irons are hot. You go ahead."

Chuck walked his horse to the far side of the pen where the mother cows and calves had congregated. Building a loop in his rope, he swung it twice and threw a trap around the hind feet of the first calf he came to. Turning his horse to the left, he pulled the slack and the loop tightened around the calf's hind legs. He then trotted toward the branding crew.

John motioned to Parker and Joe Dan to flank the heifer calf. As Chuck rode past, Joe Dan grabbed the rope near the calf's hind legs and then sat down by the calf as it lay on the ground. In one motion he took the loop off the calf's legs, and placed his right boot in the crook of the calf's bottom leg and stretched it toward the front. He held the calf's other back leg in his hands up against his body.

At the same time Parker had gone to the calf's head and put his knee on its neck while he held its top front leg bent inward to immobilize it. Once the calf was secure, Tom Smith walked up with the sizzling branding iron and applied it to its ribs. He worked it back and forth to make sure it branded evenly and when the calf's hair started to burn, he pulled it away and brushed out the flame with his boot.

The Cross L brand showed rosy pink, and Tom nodded that it met his approval. Simultaneously, John cut a long notch from the bottom of the calf's left ear with his pocketknife and then a swallow fork from the end of her right ear. Another cowboy came and inoculated the calf with a syringe gun, after which the boys stood up and let her go.

She sprang to her feet and ran back to the cattle bleating as she went, complaining to her kinsmen of the rough treatment she'd just received from the cowboys. Soon, Chuck brought another calf and the process began again, this time with a different set of flankers. The second calf was a bull so John castrated it along with marking its ears. He draped the testicle sack over a cardboard box that set next to the branding irons as he would do with the others so he could count the number of bull calves that had been castrated and branded when they were finished.

It took almost an hour to get the forty or fifty calves in the pen branded. Then they were turned out to another pen and another bunch was run in. Parker and Joe Dan kept at it, flanking every other calf. By the time a third bunch was pushed into the branding pen, they were both getting tired, but they revived when John told them to catch their horses.

They hurried to their horses and mounted, then tied the ends of their ropes to their saddle horns. When they walked into the branding pen they separated to the opposite sides and waited for John to give them the okay to start.

Parker looked over at Joe Dan and said, "Now, you be sure to give me a lot of room, because no better than you rope, I'm gonna need it to get all of these calves drug."

"Parker, I suggest you just try to stay in the middle of that old plug your ridin' and try not to fall off. It sure interrupts things when we have to stop everything just to get you back on your horse," Joe Dan replied with his usual smile.

Before Parker could reply, John called out that the irons were hot, so he built a loop and moved toward the calf closest to him. He swung the rope and threw a nice trap at the calf's hind legs, but when he started to pull his slack, the calf kicked at the loop and knocked it away. Parker muttered to himself but quietly built another loop. To make matters worse, he looked over and saw that Joe Dan had caught his calf cleanly and was already at the branding fire.

He caught his next calf, even though by just one leg. He trotted Chester to the flankers and turned him around when he got to the fence to wait for them to flank the calf and take the rope off.

"Now that we're warmed up, I think it's time to show our compadre how to throw twine," he said to Chester, and they walked back to the cattle.

He roped the next three in a row, catching each one by two feet. Problem was, Joe Dan roped just as well and had also not missed. The two boys went back and forth, bringing calves fast enough to keep four sets of flankers busy.

John looked at Parker's dad and said, "What's got into them? I don't remember them roping like that last spring."

"Beats me," Parker's dad replied. "Could be they're growing up or, knowing them, they're just trying to beat each other."

Just then, they heard a commotion. Looking toward the boys, they saw where a calf Joe Dan had caught by one leg had managed to run around his horse and had gotten the rope caught up under its tail. Centavo, usually well mannered and gentle, had started bucking toward the cattle pushed up against the far side of the pen.

Joe Dan tried to pull Centavo's head up, but the calf continued to wrap the rope around both the boy and his horse. Joe Dan stayed in the saddle until the third jump which threw him over on the left side. He grabbed the saddle horn with his right hand, but it wasn't enough to keep his momentum from almost throwing him off the horse. As the horse started another jump, James and Curtis both sprang into view. James had his pocketknife drawn and as he reached the calf, grabbed it and threw it on its side. Almost in the same motion he cut the rope to free Joe Dan and his horse.

Curtis rushed to Joe Dan and with one hand pushed the boy back into the saddle. With the other he grabbed the horse's bridle. Blood squirted from Joe Dan's nose as Curtis settled the horse. He pulled the boy from the saddle and laid him on the ground.

Joe Dan's eyes were closed. Curtis lifted his head, took his hat off, and put it under his head for a pillow. The rest of the branding crew huddled around, and Tom Smith asked, "What happened?" He hadn't seen the wreck because he had been branding on the other side of the pen.

"Oh, the darn calf ran around his horse and got the rope under his tail," said James. "That pony dang sure turned a crank."

"Yeah, I didn't think he had it in him," Parker said as he watched from his horse.

Soon, Joe Dan moved an arm, then a leg, and then opened his eyes. He shook his head and started to sit up but Curtis held him down. "Hold on, partner. You wait a minute. We need to make sure you're not hurt."

He took the handkerchief out of his back pocket and wiped the blood off of the boy's nose and face. "How'd you get a bloody nose, anyway?" He let Joe Dan sit up and gave him the handkerchief.

"Well, as far as I can remember, when he started buckin', he threw me up into my swells, and then his head came up and whacked me in the nose," Joe Dan said.

John knelt by him and said, "Let me take a look." He pulled off his glove and gently felt around Joe Dan's nose. "How bad does that hurt?"

"It's a little sore, but I don't think it's that bad," Joe Dan said as he got to his feet.

"Well, I don't think it's broken, but I imagine you'll have a pretty good shiner tomorrow."

"It's gonna take more than that to keep me from dragging the rest of these calves," Joe Dan said. He dusted himself off and said, "You guys would be all day if Parker had to do it by himself."

Everybody laughed. James brought him his horse and said, "I'm sorry I had to cut your rope. But, I thought you probably wouldn't mind."

Joe Dan shook his hand. "I sure appreciate you getting to me when you did. I was kinda in a bind."

He took the rein from James and then untied the rope from his saddle horn. "Will somebody loan me a rope? I promise not to get it cut up this time."

Everybody laughed again. Curtis stepped up and handed him a rope. Joe Dan thanked him, put it over his saddle horn, and climbed back on his horse. John picked up the boy's hat, straightened it, and dusted it off. "See if you can keep on your horse this time. We've still got a lot of calves to brand," he said smiling as he handed it to Joe Dan.

When the crew had finished branding the last of the calves, John turned off the gas to the branding pot and said, "If you men don't mind, turn 'em out in that west pasture and pair 'em up. Then we'll eat dinner."

Parker and Joe Dan caught their horses and rode out the gate with the rest of the men before the cows and calves were let out. After everyone had ridden about three hundred yards they turned and fanned out in order to keep the mother cows from going past them and either grazing or going to water without their calves.

As soon as James opened the gate, the cows moved slowly out into the pasture, bawling for their calves as they went. In turn, the calves bawled for their mothers. After about thirty minutes all of the calves had found their mothers either by means of smell or sound, and John was satisfied that everything was matched up. He signaled to the men, and they started walking their horses back to the corrals.

Parker rode up beside Joe Dan and said, "Are you okay, amigo? Your right eye's already getting pretty dark."

"It ain't that bad. But what do you think about this guy," he said as he looked down at Centavo and petted him on the neck. "I thought his pitching days were over."

"I did too, but I guess we'd do the same thing if we had a rope stretched up under our tail," Parker said with a laugh.

After the cowboys loaded the branding equipment into

the truck, they hit a buggy trot to headquarters. Everyone was in high spirits, pleased with how the branding had gone and looking forward to the lunch that the Cross L cookhouse was famous for.

James was in the lead along with Parker and Joe Dan intently talking to them. He was so engrossed in his story that he didn't notice Curtis ride up on his right side and deftly unbuckle the rear cinch of his saddle. As the cinch swung free, it snapped back and hit James' horse in the belly. The horse jumped in surprise and almost unseated the cowboy.

"What the heck?" he yelled when he got his horse pulled up. Everybody laughed. He stepped off and started looking to see what had caused his horse to jump. He turned to let everyone know he didn't think it was any too funny when he saw Curtis sitting on his horse with his arms folded, looking up into the sky and whistling.

"You son of a gun. What'd you do anyway?"

"Me? What are you talking about? Why would you think that I did something?" Curtis innocently replied.

"Because I know you," James said and started looking at his horse and saddle. Immediately he saw his unbuckled cinch. "Augh! I'll get you," he said looking at Curtis as he walked around his horse to buckle the cinch. "And I'll do it when you least expect it."

"Oh, Jimmy boy, cain't you take a joke?" Curtis said. "I was just trying to save those boys from having to listen to those windies of yours."

He rode up to James, slapped him on the back, and then hit a run toward the corrals. "Why you...," James said as he kicked up his horse in hot pursuit. When he caught up to him, they started shoving each other and laughing. James tried to unbuckle Curtis' cinch but couldn't get close enough. By the time they reached the gate, they had tears running down their eyes from laughing so hard.

"I wish we had that kind of energy," Parker's dad said to John as they watched the boys.

"I do too, but if we did, we'd probably get ourselves hurt."

When the riders got to the cook house, they either tied their horses to the hitch rack or hobbled them in the yard. They took turns washing their hands with Lava soap at the back porch sink. The two towels were black with grime after everyone had washed.

Inside the cook house, they all found spots around the long white table centered in the room next to the kitchen. Arturo, the Cross L cook, had populated the table with platters of roast beef, bowls of green and red chile, pinto beans, fried potatoes, and two stacks of fresh tortillas.

"Mr. Robles, I hope you'll take this in the right way, but none of us hardly come over here just to help you brand calves. We just come to eat Arturo's cooking," Curtis said with a smile.

"Well, I'll tell you something, the only reason I brand is so I can eat good too," John replied with his own smile.

4

THE SADDLE ORDER

Three days after the branding Parker woke when the first sun light hit his bedroom window. The morning was bright and fresh, and it made him even more excited because it was his fourteenth birthday.

He got out of bed and walked to the bathroom across the hall to start bath water. He wanted to surprise his mother and dad by cleaning up so that they wouldn't have to remind him before they went to town.

His folks always took him to town on his birthday. It had been a ritual since he was six years old. Although Parker got presents each year from his grandparents and Andy and Donnie and Joe Dan, he knew for sure that his folks would buy him a new pair of boots and two pair of Levi's at Johnson's Ranch Supply when they got to town and then take him to eat cheese enchiladas or chicken fried steak at Caralina's Café.

His friends at school liked to get music players and skateboards for their birthdays, but he didn't care about that kind of stuff. A pair of boots was about the best thing he thought he could ever get, and besides, the music on the radio was good enough for him. There weren't any sidewalks at the ranch to skateboard on anyway.

When he walked into the kitchen, his dad whistled when he saw Parker's hair combed and that he had on a clean shirt. His mother hugged him and wished him happy birthday. Even though he was fourteen, he couldn't help liking the attention.

"Sit down, honey. I made French toast and scrambled eggs for you," his mother said.

Parker smiled and sat by his dad. Tom Smith leaned toward his son and sniffed the air.

"What's that smell?" he asked. "Smells like a barber shop."

"Oh, Dad, you know it's Old Spice. I borrowed some of it out of your bathroom," Parker said.

"Well, I thought you were supposed to shave before you used after shave lotion."

"Tom, leave him alone. He'll be shaving soon enough as it is," his mother said.

When Parker finished his breakfast and drank the last of his milk, his dad pulled an envelope out of his back pocket and handed it to him.

"Happy birthday, son," he said.

"What's this?" Parker asked as he opened the envelope and pulled out a picture of a saddle from Western Horseman magazine.

His mother came over and stood by his dad. "We thought it was time you had a new saddle. You go with your Dad to see Mr. Oliver this morning and order what you want."

Parker's mouth dropped. "I can't believe it. I never would've thought you get me a saddle."

"Son, we're proud of you. We like how you keep your grades up, and how we hardly ever have to remind you to do your chores. And, besides, we wanted to get it in time so you can ride it on the 4th of July," said his Dad.

"Wow!" was all he could say as he got a faraway look on his face. He started going over in his mind what kind of saddle he would get.

When they got to Spanish Fork, Parker's dad turned off Main Street to a little street where he stopped in front of Mrs. Reed's dress shop. Parker looked at his Dad in disbelief, wondering what they were doing in front of a ladies' store when they were supposed to be at the saddle shop.

"Take it easy, son. I'm just going in to get some thread for your mother," his Dad said.

Parker said, "Okay, Dad. I guess I'm just a little anxious."

"I know you are, but I'll just be a minute."

As his Dad went inside the store, Parker picked up the Miller's Stockman catalog that his Dad had given him and started looking at saddles and figuring out what he was going to order. He already had a pretty good idea of what he wanted because one of the favorite things that he and Joe Dan ever talked about was kinds of saddles they liked.

He was deep in thought when he heard his Dad open the truck door. He smiled at him, glad he was able to get the errand done so quickly. His Dad started the truck, backed it out, and drove to Main Street and Oliver's Saddle Shop.

Almost before the truck stopped, Parker jumped out and ran into the shop ahead of his father. He went straight to Dan Oliver, the owner, who was bent over his bench carving a floral pattern on a saddle fender. The saddlemaker looked up when he heard the boy. He took off his glasses and shook the boy's hand.

"Well, what're you up to, compadre?" he asked.

"It's my birthday," the boy replied. "And I'm here to order a saddle."

Oliver laughed and said, "Well, we better hurry up and pick out some silver conchos before your Dad gets here."

"Oh, you know I don't like that kind of stuff, but I am

hoping Dad'll at least let me get the skirts basket stamped," Parker replied.

Parker's Dad walked in and shook hands with Oliver.

"I guess you're pretty upset with all the rain you've been getting," Oliver said. "I heard you even had to put off a few brandings."

"Dan, you know you'll never hear me cuss moisture, no matter what it might get in the way of," Parker's Dad said.

They continued talking, first about the price of steers, then the price of oats, and then the price of Chevrolet pickups. But the only price that mattered to Parker was the price of saddles, and the more they talked about other things, the more fidgety he got.

Finally, his Dad said with a wink in his eye, "Oh, by the way, did Parker tell you that his mother and I want to get him a saddle?"

"Well, as a matter of fact, he did mention it. But I don't suppose he has any idea of what he wants, ya think?" said Oliver.

"I sure do." Parker said and in quick order rattled off the measurements for the height of the horn, the width of the swells, and the length of the seat that he wanted.

Oliver grinned at him and said, "Slow down, partner. You better let me write some of this down."

It took thirty minutes for Parker and the saddlemaker to go over all of the measurements and particulars of the saddle that the boy wanted. When they were finished, Tom Smith could tell by the look on his son's face that he was satisfied with the way the saddle was going to turn out. Besides, Dan Oliver made the best saddles in the country and the cowboys on all of the ranches in the country wanted to ride one.

Parker decided to have brass conchos put on the saddle strings, and his Dad agreed to let him have the skirts basket-stamped even though it would make the saddle more expensive.

When they were ready to go, they shook hands with

Oliver. The saddlemaker put his hand on the boy's shoulder and said, "You know, I'm going to try to rush this along because you might just want to ride it on the 4th of July."

Parker smiled wide and shook Oliver's hand again. "That'd be great, if you think you could."

"Well, we'll see. You might want to stop in every time your mother and Dad come to town and see how I'm coming along. I'll especially want you to come in and sit in it when I start to carve the ground seat."

"You bet I will," Parker said as he and his Dad walked out the door.

As they started to walk up the street to the truck, Parker's Dad said, "You know what? All this saddle-making stuff has made me hungry. What say we go to Caralina's and get us a chicken-fried steak."

"That sound good to me," the boy replied even though he was so excited about his new saddle that he hadn't had time to get hungry or to think about food.

When they walked into Caralina's café, they found that it was almost deserted except for a few of the late morning coffee drinkers. Parker's Dad looked at the clock on the wall and said, "Well, I sure didn't think it was only 11:30, but I'm hungry anyway. How about you?"

Parker nodded, figuring that he'd be hungry once he smelled what was coming from the kitchen. They sat down at the table by the window so that they could see what was going on out on the street. Soon Caralina emerged from the kitchen. She was an attractive Hispanic lady who wore her long, black hair pulled back on her head where it hung almost to her waist. As usual, she wore a flower print dress and leather sandals. Her smile was bright as she said, "Buenas dias, cowboys. What are working men doing in town on a Tuesday?"

Parker didn't hesitate in telling her about his new saddle. But before he got too far along, his Dad interrupted and said,

"Son, we can always bring it over when it's finished so Caralina can see it. But why don't we go ahead and order before she gets very busy."

Parker said, "Oh, sorry. I guess I'm just a little excited."

"That's all right, muchacho. A man's first saddle made for him is an important thing, and he should be excited," Caralina said.

Parker couldn't help smiling when she referred to him as being a man.

Before he could say anything, his Dad said, "Caralina, let us have two chicken fried steaks, and I guess you'd better bring us a couple of pieces of cherry pie before we get out of here."

"And that pie's going to be on me to celebrate," Caralina said as she turned to go to the kitchen.

Caralina's café was one of Parker's favorite places in Spanish Fork. She had been cooking for the area's ranchers and cowboys for more than twenty years. Her two daughters had grown up in the café, waitressing through high school, and now, even though they were married and living in the next county, they came home every chance they got to help her out.

The café was lined with knotty pine paneling and had an eating counter that ran along the back wall. The round shiny steel stools in front of it were covered with red plastic as were the chairs that sat around the tables. The most impressive thing to Parker about Caralina's was the pictures that she had hung on the walls. She had all of the cowboy favorites, Charlie Russell, Frederick Remington, and Will James, and every time they came in for a burger or a bowl of chile, they always spent time looking at them and discussing the merits of each one.

Before long, Caralina came out with their chicken-fries. Suddenly, Parker found he was hungry, and he dug in as fast as he could. His Dad reminded him to eat slower and to put his napkin in his lap. Parker did as he was told, but all he could really think about was that, next to his mother, Caralina made the best mashed potatoes and gravy in the whole country.

When they'd finished their meals, Caralina brought their cherry pie and poured more coffee for Parker's Dad and filled up Parker's milk glass. After a few bites, Parker said to himself that maybe Caralina's cherry pie was even better than his mother's, but he decided not to say anything to his Dad. He would hate it if his Dad kidded him about it in front of his mother because it might hurt her feelings.

Parker's Dad paid the check and left Caralina a tip that more than made up for the cost of the pie. They told her goodbye, and she made Parker promise to bring in his saddle whenever it was finished.

They walked to the truck and Parker's Dad drove west on Commerce Street before he turned left on Capitol to catch the highway south that led to the ranch twenty miles away. It was warm in the truck, and Parker sat next to the open window and thought about his new saddle and what it would look like cinched on Chester. His last thought before he dozed off was how good they were going to look riding in the parade on the 4th of July.

5

PROWLING THE MANUELAS

The Friday after his birthday, Parker was out early working to touch his colt and getting him gentle. Each successive time Parker worked with the colt, he got to be more comfortable with the boy putting his hands on him.

After Parker turned the mare and colt loose, he ran to the house to tell his mother how well things were going with the colt. She wasn't in the kitchen when he walked in, but he saw a plate of oatmeal cookies she'd left for him on the table with a note saying that she had gone to visit with Mrs. Klein over at the Slash O, and that his dad had gone to town for a cattlemen's meeting.

Parker got a glass out of the cupboard, poured a glass of milk, and sat down at the table to eat a few cookies. While he was eating, the telephone rang. It was Andy, one of the cowboys who worked for them, calling on his cell phone.

"Parker, do you want to go with me to prowl the Manuelas?" he asked.

"Sure. When are you going?" Parker replied.

"Just as soon as you get your horse saddled. I already turned him in for you. I just finished unloading the horse feed they delivered yesterday, and before your dad left, he asked me to check on the cows we put in the Manuelas last week when I was through," Andy said.

"I'll be right out," Parker said. He gulped down his milk and put the glass in the dishwasher. As he walked by the kitchen table, he grabbed the cookie plate and poured the cookies into a paper sack he got off the counter. "I wouldn't want 'em to go to waste," he said to himself.

He put on his hat and ran out to the corrals. It made him feel good that Andy had asked him to go. Besides Donnie Jeffers who worked for the CS Ranch, Andy Akers was his favorite of all of the cowboys in the country. Like Donnie, he had come out of Texas to punch cows in the mountains. He wasn't very tall, about 5' 8," but a lot stronger than he looked. He showed that when he loaded hay.

One of the things that Parker liked best about Andy was how well he took care of stock, whether it was horses or cattle. It was like he always made sure they were in good shape, not so much because it was his job, but just because he liked them and really cared about them. Most cowboys he knew were diligent about taking care of the animals in their charge, but it didn't seem they were devoted to them the way Andy was.

The other interesting thing about Andy to Parker was how well he took care of his hats and boots. Whereas he seemed indifferent to the condition of his saddle, ropes, and bridles, he always made sure his boots were oiled and had good soles and heels. Most of the cowboys liked high heels to ride in, but Andy's were always the highest, so much so that the heel caps on several of his boots were only as big around as a silver dollar. He told Parker that he needed them that high so that he wouldn't get hung up in a stirrup, but, without saying so, Parker knew it was just an example of Andy's cowboy vanity.

Likewise with his hats. He was always messing with his hat to make sure the brim was just the way he wanted it. Sometimes he even brushed his hat with a sponge he'd bought special for the purpose. And he always kept his town hat in the box so it wouldn't get dusty. Most everybody Parker knew just left their hats alone once they were first shaped and let nature, or tree limbs, or broncs shape them however they might. Aside from not setting them down on the brim and or laying them on a bed which was bad luck, most cowboys didn't give their hats much thought.

In spite of those idiosyncrasies, Andy was a good hand and was probably the best with a young horse of all of the cowboys his age that Parker knew. He and Andy had already talked a lot about starting Rusty and more or less the way Parker ought to go about it.

As usual, Josie was trailing Parker at his heels as he stepped up to the saddle house. He grabbed a halter and went and caught Chester. By the time he had him saddled, Andy rode up on a three-year-old colt he'd started the year before.

"If we find anything to doctor, you'll just have to do it yourself. I don't think ol' Lefty's up to the challenge yet," he said as he slid off the colt.

"That's fine with me. I just hope all the misses are out of my rope after branding season," Parker joked at himself.

Parker untied the halter from Chester's head, took it off, and retied it around his neck. He then slipped his bridle bit into his horse's mouth and hung the headstall over his head. He reached over Chester and took the right rein and draped it over the horse's neck. Finally he tightened the cinch to his saddle and turned the horse around.

Both cowboys got on their horses and went out the

headquarters gate that led toward the foothills of the San Mateo Mountains west of the ranch. Manuelas Canyon ran twenty miles into the mountains and dropped out of them about five miles from the ranch.

As they rode along, they talked about a lot of things, anything from saddles and colts to girls and baseball. Andy was as big of a baseball fan as Parker was and they both liked to watch the Colorado Rockies when they played on Saturday afternoons. Because Andy didn't have a TV in the bunkhouse, Parker always invited him over to watch the games. In addition, Andy tried to be in the stands of as many of Parker's games at school as he could.

When they got to the Manuelas gate, Andy stepped off and opened it so they could walk their horses through. After he shut the gate, he pointed to the left and said, "Parker, if you don't mind, ride those benches on that side of the creek, and I'll do the same on this side. That's where we ought to find most of them. I really hope we don't have to go all the way to the head of the canyon."

He pulled out the herd book from his front pocket and flipped through a few pages. He found the page he was looking for and after studying it for a minute, he said, "There should be three hundred and forty head in here, so as soon as we get a good count, we can go home."

"Great," Parker said, "I'll see you in a little while."

He reined Chester into the cottonwoods that ran along the creek and with Josie trotting behind crossed to the other side. When he got to the first bench, he found a cow trail that went to the top. He noticed it was pretty well traveled and so figured it must lead to some good grass.

He pointed Chester up the trail and with little effort the horse scrambled to the top. Once there Parker let his horse catch his breath and then reined him to the left where he saw three mother cows and their calves standing next to a stand of piñon trees. They were turned toward him, looking at him in dumb amazement as if they had never seen such a creature as a man on a horse before.

They stood there in their silence until Parker and Chester got beside them. Parker whistled and shushed them to get them to walk off so he could take a look at them. Woken from their trance, they started toward the downhill side of the bench at a low trot. Parker followed them for a few yards and then let them go. He turned and rode along the trees on the uphill side of the bench so that he could look into any openings that he might find. Before long he found seventeen more pair.

He felt good about how many cattle he had found on the first bench and couldn't help whistling to himself. Up ahead he saw a big break in the trees to the left, and he kicked Chester into a trot thinking there ought to be quite a few cattle there.

When he reached the opening, he pulled Chester up and turned him onto a trail between two ponderosa trees. As he passed through them he was surprised that he didn't immediately see any cattle. Nevertheless, he continued on enjoying the sunshine and the spicy smell of the junipers as they heated in the late morning sun. By the way he was traveling, Chester seemed to be liking the ride just as well.

As he rode along Parker looked down and decided he needed to rewrap the strap around his rope. As he was doing so Chester rounded a big piñon tree and suddenly stopped in his tracks. He craned his neck and pricked his ears toward a spot in the trees thirty yards away.

"What in the world," Parker said to himself as he nudged the horse forward with his spurs.

Before he had gone far, he heard a low snort in the direction of where Chester had been looking. He looked closer and on the other side of a fallen tree he saw what had gotten his horse's interest, a sow bear and two cubs. They were so intent on cleaning ants from the log that they hadn't seen Parker ride up until the wind shifted, and the mother caught the scent of the boy and the horse.

She turned slowly to look at them and was obviously annoyed at being interrupted while eating her lunch. Her twins stopped eating also and sat motionless on each side of her with their ears pointed forward. The one on the left was cinnamon colored while the other was jet black like its mother.

"Darn, I've never seen twins before," Parker said to himself wishing he had his mother's camera along. He sat on his horse looking at them for a few minutes and then reined to the right out of their way. As he got to the other side of the park he turned in his saddle and saw that the mother and cubs had returned to their mid-day meal, proving that it was far more important to them than the boy and his horse.

He walked his horse a few more steps and then suddenly pulled Chester to a stop. "Where in the heck is Josie?" he asked himself as he turned to look for her. He had been so intent on finding cattle and looking at bears that he had lost track of her.

He whistled, knowing that that was usually all it took to get her to come. He waited a few minutes and then whistled again. When she didn't come, he said to himself, "Now that's strange. She must have got into something."

Parker turned Chester around and trotted across the park to where he had come into it once again giving the mother and her cubs plenty of room. They were what got him to thinking about Josie in the first place because he knew she probably would have gotten pretty excited had she seen them the first time.

Right when he came out onto the bench Chester pricked his ears and turned his head to the right. Parker looked in the same direction and saw Josie lying on the ground with her head between her paws underneath a juniper tree. He whistled to her and she looked up for a second, but then sheepishly put head down again.

Parker spurred into a lope and by the time he was twenty yards away, he saw what was wrong with her. Her forlorn look told it all. He'd seen it before.

He slowed to a walk and stopped when he got in front of the dog. He stepped off and bent down to look at her more closely. She raised her head to look at him and proved that he was right. She had about twenty porcupine quills sticking out of her face. Like she'd done several times before, she'd found one of the prickly devils and her curiosity got the better of her. The result was she got swatted by his tail.

Josie whimpered as he petted her head. "What have I told you about porcupines?" he scolded her softly. "You need to try to learn to leave them alone. They get you every time."

After he petted her some more, he put her head back between her paws and went back to his horse. He fished a pair of pliers out of his saddle pockets and walked back to her side.

"Well, let's get this over with as soon as we can. We've still got more cattle to look at."

He sat down beside her and gently pulled her head into his lap. And then laughing he said, "Now you know this is going to hurt me more than it is you, but we've got to do it."

Josie squirmed each time Parker pulled a quill out, but because he had done it before, he was able to get them all out quickly so as not to prolong her misery. Several times she pulled her head away and rubbed her face with her paws to get relief from the pain.

When the boy finished pulling out all of the quills he could find, he gently stroked her head and said, "Now, I hope to goodness that you don't do that again, but I think I remember telling you that the last time you did it." She returned his gentleness with her usual look of devotion.

She got to her feet when he did, but he quickly saw she wasn't anywhere as frisky as she had been when they'd started that morning. Still, she felt better and fell in after him when he went to get on his horse. After a few hundred yards she was almost in her usual playful step again.

Parker finished riding out the bench and found almost fifty more head of cows. He looked for a place to drop off to go back down into the canyon, but he couldn't find a trail he thought he could get down, so he decided to lope back to where he had come up.

When he came to the spot where Josie had tangled with the porcupine, Parker looked back to check on her. Sure enough he saw her slyly start to angle to the same spot. Parker whistled and said, "Haven't you had enough of him? You come on."

Josie reluctantly obeyed although she couldn't help looking back at her prickly friend. "I've never seen a dog as intrigued by porcupines as you. It's not a very good habit, and I want you to get over it," he scolded her.

The next two hours were uneventful and by the time he came to the head of his side of the canyon, both he and Chester were tired. He had counted more than half of the cattle that were supposed to be in the canyon, and he hoped that Andy had seen the other half so that they could start back as soon as they met up.

He led Chester to the bottom of the canyon and found a spring that trickled out of the north side. It was shaded by a big cottonwood tree and several cedars and most of the rocks surrounding it were covered with moss. He stepped off and drank a few hands full of water before he let Chester drink. Of course, Josie got to drink along side of him.

As he started to get back on his horse, he heard a rustle in the trees to his left and saw Andy ride into sight as he plunged through a pair of closely set piñon trees. He smiled when he saw Parker and asked, "How'd you do?"

"I counted one hundred and seventy-seven head, and they were all in as good of shape as I think I've ever seen them," Parker said knowingly.

"Well, now let's see," Andy said as he pulled out his herd book. He took the short pencil out of his shirt pocket, licked the lead, and starting making calculations on one of the blank pages in the back.

"If you saw a hundred and seventy-seven, and if there are supposed to be three hundred and forty in here, then that means that I should have seen ...," "he paused as he did his subtraction, "a hundred and sixty-three." After checking another page of the book, he smiled and said, "And that's exactly how many I did. Now, ain't that just a wonder. I hardly ever get a right count the first time. Compadre, if you don't have any objections, I say we go home."

"You won't get any fight out of me," Parker said. Besides being tired, he was hungry. The cookies hadn't lasted very long, and because Andy was like most cowboys and refused to carry any kind of food on his saddle. Parker hadn't anything to eat in what to him was a long time.

They turned down the canyon and it took Parker almost till they got to the gate to tell Andy about his encounters with the wildlife. This time he stepped off to open the gate and after he closed it, they hit a buggy trot for home. He was excited to tell his parents the same stories too.

6

THE NEW SADDLE

It was 9:30 in the morning and a week before the 4th of July. Parker was down at the barn with a bucket of baseballs working on his throw to second base. He sat in a crouch with his mask on behind a home plate that Andy had found for him from who knows where.

Taking a ball in his glove as if he had just received it, Parker sprang out of his crouch and fired as hard as he could at a tire that hung from the walnut tree next to the barn. The tire was only a few inches off of the ground so that if he threw the ball inside of it, if would more or less simulate where he should deliver it for either the shortstop and second baseman to tag out a runner trying to steal second.

He thought to himself how lucky he was to have Josie when he practiced his second base throws. She faithfully retrieved each ball he threw, no matter how errant it might be, and returned it to him, most of the time into the plastic bucket that Parker kept on his right side.

After about every tenth ball that Josie retrieved, Parker

stopped and let her catch her breath. He'd have her sit by him and scratch her behind the ears and tell her what a good dog she was. When Josie heard Parker talk that way, she melted and her face showed more contentment than if he'd thrown her a steak bone.

When Parker had almost thrown his allotment of fifty balls, he heard the screen door slam at the back of the house. He stood up and turned to see who it was. In the morning sunshine he saw that it was his mother as she stepped through the back yard gate. He couldn't help thinking how pretty she was for a mom, dressed like she was in a calico dress. Every once in a while his friends said the same thing, although never directly to Parker, knowing he wouldn't want to hear them saying too much, good or bad, about his mother.

He watched his mother as she walked quickly toward him. She had a smile on her face so he knew something was up, and that it was probably good.

"Son, Mr. Oliver just called and said your saddle's ready," she called out to him before she was half way across the ranch yard.

When he realized what she'd said, a rush of adrenaline coursed through his body. "Hot dog!" he shouted, although he probably would have said something else if his mother hadn't been there.

He pulled off his mask and grabbed the bucket of balls and set them with his glove inside the barn door. He ran to his mother who had stopped next to the barn with the smile still on her face.

"Yeah, he just called and said you can come get it whenever you want. Isn't it a shame we weren't planning on going to town until the fourth," she said, turning her head so Parker couldn't see the grin on her face.

"Oh, Mom, are you kidding?" Parker said in disbelief. "I've

been waiting for a month for that saddle. Can't we just go in and get it anyway?"

Then he looked at her more closely and noticed she was avoiding his eyes. When he reached for her shoulder to pull her around so that she'd have to look at him, she broke out laughing. "Oh, I guess we could if you really want to," she said as she pulled him into her arms and hugged him.

"Well, then, let's go," he said as he broke away and started running to the house. Inside, he changed into a clean blue shirt and his best pair of boots. He figured, knowing his mother, that she'd want to take pictures, and he wanted to be dressed right.

When he walked out of his room and into the kitchen, his mother already had her pocket book in her hand and was putting on her sun glasses. Parker remarked to himself that if he didn't know any better, his mother was just as excited as he was.

They walked out to the white truck that was parked on the west side of the house. It was the one that Parker's dad and Andy used to feed cattle in the winter and was the only vehicle available since Parker's father had taken the ranch truck and trailer so he could ride through the mother cows and calves that had been put in the McNabb Pasture for the summer.

Parker hadn't gone with his dad because he had been asked to mow the lawn. Besides, his Dad didn't think it would take more than a couple of hours to see the cattle, so he told Parker he might as well get his mowing done while there was a chance. After the 4th of July Tom would be needing Parker pretty steady when they would have to gather the bulls and separate them from the mother cows.

"Want me to drive?" Parker asked, grinning at his mother. "No, young man, if I'm not mistaken, a person must have a valid driver's license to operate a vehicle in this state, and the last time I checked you don't have one."

"Well, you know I drive all the time," Parker said.

"Yes, I do. But that's here on the ranch. You're just going to have to wait until you're old enough."

"Well, okay. I was just trying to be helpful," Parker said with a sly grin, feeling it wasn't necessary to tell his mother he'd already driven on the highway with his dad.

"I know you were. But I think I can manage without you just fine," Parker's mother said as she opened the door to the pickup and climbed in.

The dash of the truck was layered with a fine coat of dust everywhere there wasn't either a pair of fencing pliers, a wad of binder's twine, or some worn out gloves. Parker's mother gave the messy truck one of her looks as she settled in and put the key into the ignition.

The Ford started immediately, and she put it in first gear and drove out of the ranch yard. Parker wished she would drive a little faster on the dirt road that led to the highway, but she instead slowed down at every chug hole and rock that she came to. But once she turned onto the pavement, she didn't disappoint him. She might have even exceeded the speed limit for most of the trip to town.

Parker was glad that she drove directly to the saddle shop instead of doing errands of one sort or the other first. There were a couple of trucks parked in front of Oliver's when they got there, and they had to park almost at the end of the block. Parker really wanted to run as fast as he could to the front door, but he knew it wouldn't look right. And besides he knew his mother would give him a talking to if he didn't wait for her.

When they walked in the door, Parker's heart sank. Not only were there three people already there, but one of them, a red headed cowboy who worked for the Rafter J, was sitting in a saddle tree, looking very much like he was ordering a saddle. "This is gonna take a while, I betcha. Just my luck," Parker said to himself.

But miraculously, when Dan Oliver looked up and saw

Parker and his mother walk in, he excused himself and walked up to them with a big smile on his face. He shook hands with Parker and innocently asked, "Can I help you with something, son?"

"Wull, yeah! I came for my saddle," Parker said.

"Oh, well let me go see if it's ready," Oliver said as he winked at Ann Smith. Parker turned and looked at his mother in disbelief. But when he saw the expression on her face, he could tell they were just having fun with him, if you wanted to call it fun. When he looked back around, both Oliver and his mother burst out laughing.

"Okay, son, I'll bring it right out. I can't wait for you to see how it turned out," Oliver said.

In a few minutes he was back carrying Parker's new rig. It seemed to glisten as he set it on a stand. "Might as well mount up," he said.

Parker didn't hesitate. He put his boot in the left stirrup and swung his right leg over. "Boy, it feels good," he said after he had settled into both stirrups.

"Wow, now that's a rigging," said the red headed cowboy who had come over to watch. "Mr. Oliver, I'm thinking I want one just like that."

It made Parker feel good to hear that a cowboy older than he was would want a saddle like his. He stepped off so that he could stand off and get a better look at it. He then looked around for his mother. She was on her cell phone and had a worried look on her face. In the excitement over his new saddle, he hadn't even noticed that her cell phone had rung.

"Who is it?" he asked. She raised her hand to let him know to wait until she hung up. When she took the phone from her ear and closed it, she looked concerned, but calmly said, "Son, load your saddle. Andy just called and said that Dad must have got bucked off because his horse just showed up at the house without him. I want you to go with Andy and find him."

Without saying anything, Parker turned and shook Oliver's hand. He then picked up his saddle and headed for the door.

"I'm sorry, Dan, but we better go check on Tom," his mother said. "We'll come back in tomorrow and pay you." She followed her son out the door.

7

FINDING TOM

A million things went through Parker's mind as his mother turned onto the highway that led to the ranch. He just hoped his Dad was all right, and that he hadn't broken anything or worse.

His mother saw the concern on his face and reached over and squeezed his arm. "We'll find him, son," she said.

When they got to the ranch, Andy was standing in front of the saddle house holding the reins to one of his horses and Chester. Both were saddled. Before Parker's mother had fully stopped the truck, the boy jumped out and ran to the corral.

When he got up to Andy he started sputtering questions as fast as he could. "When did his horse get here? Where did he go? Why did he even take a trailer? Isn't anybody else going to help us? Who di..."

"Hold on there partner. One question at a time," Andy said. "I don't know why he took a trailer being that he was only going to the McNabb. I guess he was in a hurry. But it doesn't matter. We just need to find him. His horse showed up about two hours ago."

They mounted their horses and while Andy was opening the swinging gate that led into the horse pasture, they heard a whistle from the lane in front of the house.

"Hey, wait for me." They turned and saw Joe Dan riding in on Centavo. When he got to them he said, "Your mom called my mom and told her what happened. I caught my horse as soon as I heard. I'm just glad I got here in time to go with you."

"Thanks, buddy," Parker said sincerely. "He shouldn't be too hard to find. He just went over to the McNabb."

All three kicked their horses into a lope. When they reached the far side of the horse pasture and went through the gate, they reined to the right and headed east. They only had to cross one pasture in order to reach the McNabb.

"Your dad must have left this gate open when he went across. How else could his horse have gotten home? I'm really surprised the horse left him, as much feed that's in there," Andy said.

"Who knows? It all sounds pretty peculiar," Parker replied.

They were at the gate of the McNabb within thirty minutes. It was set next to a stand of junipers which blocked their view to the rest of the pasture. After they went through the gate, they rode around the trees and saw Tom Smith's truck and trailer about fifty feet away with the trailer gate open. They trotted over, and Andy and Parker got off their horses.

"Well, the tracks show he headed to the windmill, which is where you'd expect him to go," said Andy. "Parker, if you don't mind, go back to the gate and see if you can see any tracks."

He got back on his horse and started walking with Joe Dan alongside where Tom had ridden toward the windmill. Parker led his horse to the gate and saw a set of horse tracks headed out in the soft ground. Underneath the tracks their horses just laid down, Tom Smith's horse looked like he had gone through the gate in a high trot.

"Darn. I wonder what happened to my dad," the boy said

to himself. He got back on his horse and kicked him into a lope to catch up with Andy and Joe Dan.

When he got to them, he said, "Yeah. I saw tracks, and it looks like his horse was going at a pretty fast clip when he went through."

"Okay," Andy said. "Let's get after it. He's got to be in here somewhere, and we need to find him before it gets dark."

They trotted their horses as much as they could as they followed the tracks slowing down only when they got to rocky places. The McNabb pasture was one of the biggest on the ranch and even though it looked like Tom had gone to check the windmill first, from then on there was no telling where he could have gone.

When they got to the windmill, Andy stopped his horse about twenty yards away and got off. He motioned for the boys to hold up. "Let me have a look see first so we don't mess up any tracks."

He handed Joe Dan the reins to his horse and started walking toward the windmill with his eyes on the ground. "Yeah, here's where he rode in. And then it looks like he circled around once. He must have just wanted to see if it was pumping good because his horse's tracks are on top of the cattle's. There probably wasn't anything here when he got here."

Andy walked off to the west and then came back and started to circle the tank. Soon, he waved and called to the boys, "Here's where he rode off," pointing to a grove of scrub oaks and junipers to the north. "Let's go."

The boys rode up, and Andy got on his horse and led them in a trot toward the trees. The sun was setting behind Lone Star Peak in the west, but they would still have more than an hour-and-a-half before it got dark.

Suddenly, Andy pulled up his horse and turned to the boys. "You know, when I pulled the saddle off your dad's horse, I didn't see his rope on the horn. I wonder if he tried to rope something and got himself into a jackpot."

"Well, that could explain it. For an old guy he still likes to rope a bunch," Parker said after they had kicked back into a trot.

When they got to the junipers, they came to a cow trail that went around the trees and saw Tom's horse's tracks alongside. On the other side, they saw him. He was sitting leaning against a cottonwood tree with his hat off and his head bent down on his chest.

All three riders kicked into a lope and slid their horses to a stop almost at the man's feet. Andy got to him first and immediately grabbed his left arm to check for a pulse.

"He's alive, at least," he said to the boys. "I feel his pulse and can hear him breathing. I think he just passed out."

He started feeling around the man's body to see if he could tell if he had anything broken. "It doesn't look like he's got anything broke but that bump on his head looks pretty nasty. Joe Dan, get the slickers, and let's lay him down."

Joe Dan started back to the horses, but before he got to them, he shouted, "What in the world?"

Parker and Andy looked up to where Joe Dan pointed. About thirty yards away next to a cholla cactus, they saw a coyote lying on its side with its head turned back in an unnatural position. When they looked closer, they saw that it had a lariat rope around its neck.

"Well, that could explain it. It looks like your dad was taking a little roping practice on that coyote and got himself in trouble doing it," Andy said to Parker.

Parker shook his head. "I know he's my dad but you'd think at his age he would've given up trying to rope wildlife. At least he ought to make sure he's got someone with him when he does."

Parker's comment caused Andy to chuckle under his breath. "Now who's the adult and who's the teenager here?" he laughed.

When Joe Dan brought the slickers, Andy spread one of them on the ground next to Tom. Although he was still unconscious, he was breathing normally so they carefully lifted him and laid him on his back on the slicker. Parker rolled up another slicker and put it under his dad's head.

"Well, what should we do?" Parker asked.

"I don't rightly know. Too bad we can't get cell phone service out here. We could at least call your mom," Andy replied.

The three squatted on their boot heels looking first at Tom and then at each other. Before long they heard a groan come from the prostrate man and then saw him open his eyes, shake his head, and attempt to sit up. Andy leaned over and held him down so he couldn't.

"Take it easy, Tom. Can you hear me?" Andy asked.

Tom focused his eyes on Andy and rubbed the back of his head. "Whew, I've got a heck of a headache. What're you guys doing here?"

"Looking for you," Parker said. "Mom and I were in town picking up my saddle when Andy called and said your horse had showed at the house without you. What in the heck happened?"

"Well, now I don't really know," Tom said as he closed his eyes with a grimace. His speech showed that he was still groggy. Finally, he opened his eyes and said, "Let me sit up."

Andy got behind him and lifted him up so he could lean against the cottonwood tree. He sat there a minute as his mind cleared, ever once in a while looking from one boy to other. After a bit, he asked, "Did I catch the coyote?"

"You sure did," Andy replied. "But what were you doing trying to rope a coyote out here by yourself?"

"Well, I guess I just thought that since he was so close when I saw him, I ought to teach him a lesson for being around my calves. But, then Lucky stepped in a gopher hole right as I was about to throw and dumped me on my head. I didn't even see if I caught."

"All I know is that I hit hard, and I guess it knocked me out. I don't know how long I layed out, and when I finally woke up, I didn't know where I was. I do remember being able to get up and walking over here, but then I guess I passed out again once I got here."

"Dad, I hate to tell ya, but you're not twenty-five anymore," Parker said as he got up to get his dad's hat.

"I guess I keep forgetting, huh? Mother's probably not going to be all that proud of me when she hears about this," Tom said with a sheepish grin.

"Joe Dan, would you go get the truck? I think you ought to be able to drive right to us. We'll put him in and go have his head looked at," Andy said.

Once they had him in the truck, Andy gave him some aspirin he found in the glove box. They loaded the horses and started for the ranch. When they were out on the flats, Andy saw that he had a cell phone signal so he gave the phone to Parker so he could call his mother.

When she answered the phone, he said, "Well, we found him and, he's all right, just a little banged up."

"What'd he do?" she asked with concern in her voice.

"He had a little accident trying to rope something, but it looks like he's going to be all right. He hit his head pretty hard when he fell off his horse so I think we ought to go have him checked out."

"Well, what do you mean pretty hard?" she asked excitedly. "Let me talk to him."

"Mom, actually he's sleeping right now, and I don't think we ought to wake him up. We'll explain everything when we get home. Just don't worry, he's going to be all right."

When she hung up the phone, Parker's mother called Dr. Thompson in town and told him what she knew.

"Well, just in case I'm going to drive out and take a look at him. I don't like it when cowboys fall on their head."

"Thanks, Doc. We'll be waiting for you. They should almost be here."

Parker mother's told herself to stay calm. She busied herself by putting on a pot of coffee and making sandwiches. When she finished, she turned on the yard light so that they could see once they drove in and then sat on the porch straining her eyes to see truck headlights.

In about fifteen minutes she saw them driving in. She ran out the yard gate and waited anxiously for Andy to stop the truck. When Parker opened his door, she hugged him and asked, "How is he?"

"Oh, he's all right. He just now woke up."

Before she could say anything, Tom said from the back seat, "Honey, I'm all right. I've just got a little headache."

"What did you do?" she asked, relieved to see that he appeared to be okay.

"Ah, nothing much, my horse fell with me right when I was trying to rope."

"Tom, you know I don't like you trying to doctor when you're by yourself. Was it a cow or a calf?" she asked.

"Well, that's kind of the problem. It was a coyote."

"What!" and she knew not to go any further with the kids there. "Come on, let's get you inside. Doc Thompson will be here any minute."

As she helped him out of the back seat, she told the boys they could go unsaddle their horses. "I think I can get him in okay."

Once Andy drove off, she hugged her husband and said, "When are you ever going to learn? We can't afford to have you hurt. Sometimes you do things like you did before we got married."

"I know, Parker already reminded me. But I didn't think it was a big deal because that coyote was pretty close, and I was mad at him because I could tell he'd been messing with my calves."

"Well, next time, you just wait on some help when you think you've got to administer your kind of range justice," she said as she smiled at him. "Now let's go lay you down and see what the doctor says."

8

THE 4ᵀᴴ OF JULY

Parker woke before day break on the morning of the 4th of July. He took a shower and put on a white shirt like all of the other cowboys wore on rodeo day. He stuck his pants legs into his red-top boots and went to the kitchen where his Dad was drinking coffee and his mother was mixing pancakes.

"Morning," he said, "Happy 4th of July, everybody." His parents returned his greeting with a smile. Before his Dad had a chance to say anything, Parker said, "If you don't mind, I'll go feed the horses and hook up the trailer before breakfast. Who do you want to ride?" he asked his Dad.

His Dad looked up from the cattleman's magazine he was reading. He had recovered quickly from his roping accident. Even though he was also excited about the day, he couldn't help but chuckle at his son's enthusiasm.

"Well, I think ol' Jake'll do," he replied. "And, if you don't mind, go ahead and put my Oliver saddle on him. I want him to look as good as Chester in the parade."

Parker smiled back and put on his black hat as he went out the door. The sun was coming up over Saddle Back Mountain east of the house when he got to the corral gate where Josie was waiting for him. As usual, he scratched her behind the ears.

The saddle horses were also waiting for him in the horse trap on the other side of the corral. He opened the gate for them and then ran across the corral and opened the gate that went into the saddle house pen. He got two feed bags from the saddle house and filled them with oats. He hung them from his shoulders and walked back to the gate where Chester was waiting. After the big horse walked through, he turned around and let Parker hang the bag on his head.

Parker turned back to the gate and looked under the top rail to find his dad's horse, Jake. He was with the other horses in the middle of the big pen standing by the grain feeder waiting patiently for his breakfast.

Parker whistled, and Jake threw up his head and pointed his ears at the boy. He walked over, and Parker let him into the pen. With feed bags on both horses, Parker ran to his dad's white flatbed pickup that was parked in front of the house, started it, and drove over to their best stock trailer.

He pulled around to the front and backed up to the hitch. When he was about two feet away, he stopped, put the truck in park, and got out to see how well he was lined up. He discovered that the ball was three inches to the left side, so he got back in and turned the front wheels to the right. He slowly went back until he heard the clink of the hitch hitting the ball. Again he got out and saw that he only needed to push the trailer over a bit so that the hitch would drop on the ball.

When he had everything secure, he drove the truck and trailer in front of the corrals and went to saddle the horses. After he pulled the feed bags off the horses and put halters on them, he combed and brushed each one. He then pulled his Dad's flower carved saddle that Dan Oliver had made from its rack along with the blankets, and walked out and cinched it on Jake.

When he was through, he stepped back and gave the horse a critical look. He agreed with his Dad that Jake did look good under the rigging.

But now was the time he'd been waiting for because he was finally going to get to put his own new saddle on Chester. In the hustle and bustle of the last week with his dad getting hurt, he hadn't even taken the time to ride it.

He walked slowly to the saddle house, relishing the moment. Once inside, he pulled the saddle from its rack, grabbed his blanket and headed back to his horse. He let his horse smell the saddle and then let him admire it, knowing full well his horse was just as proud of it as he was.

He positioned the blanket on Chester's back and swung the saddle on. He cinched him up loose and then untied the halter and led his horse to the center of the corral. He dropped the lead rope and stepped back to take a look. Chester stood with his head turned toward the boy. Parker couldn't believe how good everything looked, his horse, his saddle, everything.

"I've got to get a picture of this," he said to himself and turned to run to the house. But to his surprise, his mother was walking up with her camera in her hand.

"Mind if I get a picture?" she asked, smiling at him.

"I was just coming to get you," Parker replied as he ran to hug her.

"First, let me take a few of Chester by himself, and then I'll get some of you," she said.

Parker couldn't help but grin. When he went to the saddle house to get his bridle, he had a smile that stayed on his face all the time his mother was taking pictures. It surprised his mother because he was like his father and usually didn't smile in front of cameras, even though he smiled everywhere else.

After his mother went back to the house, Parker got Jake's bridle from the saddle house and hung it on his saddle horn. He took off Chester's bridle and put his halter back on. As a precaution, he went to each horse and tied the near side saddle string around the bridles so that they couldn't shake them off while they were in the trailer.

He led both horses out of the pen and loaded them. At the yard gate he met his dad. "I've already eaten, son. You go ahead. I'm gonna get the tarp out of the barn so we can set it up for mother on the south side of the arena. Mom's frying chicken for lunch," his dad said over his shoulder as he continued toward the corrals.

Parker went in the back door, hung up his hat, and sat at the kitchen table. His mother smiled at him and reached for the bowl of batter and poured four pancakes onto the griddle.

"What are you going to enter today?" she asked.

"The ribbon roping with Kelly and the cowpony race," Parker said as he started on his pancakes. Then he looked up at his mother and said, "And probably the steer riding."

She turned around and asked, "The steer what?"

"Yeah, ah, I thought I'd ride a steer this year. It ain't no big deal, Mom," he replied.

"Says who? It may not a big deal to you, but it is to me," she said. "Have you talked with your father?"

"Well, kinda. He said it'd be all right with him if it was all right with you."

"Well, I don't know. I don't know what I'd do if you got hurt riding something that didn't need riding," she said.

"Oh, Mom, don't worry. Besides, they plowed the arena the other day, and it's as soft as a feather bed," Parker said.

"I bet it is," his mother said as she walked to the table and put her arm around him. "I don't care how soft it is. We've got enough stock right here to where you don't need to go to town to fall off something. You better just wait until next year."

Parker dropped his head trying to think of something he could say to his mother to get her to change her mind. But then he quickly decided it probably wasn't worth getting in an argument with his mother on rodeo day, so he looked up and said, "Well, okay. But next year for sure."

His mother smiled at him and said, "That'll be fine, but for what it's worth, it'll just make me feel better today knowing I don't have to worry about you getting bucked off something."

He went back to eating his pancakes trying to eat as slow as he could, but he found he wasn't being very successful. He was too excited. When he finally gulped his last bite and finished his milk, he took his dishes to the sink and hugged his mother.

"See you in town, Mom. Love ya," he said over his shoulder as he dashed out the door to meet his dad at the truck.

9

DONNIE

On the way to town Parker and his dad saw a herd of antelope in the pasture that the WS Ranch owned next to the highway that went to Spanish Fork.

"There's so many of those goats around here that they'll be grazing the lawns in town before you know it," his dad said.

Parker liked it that there was so much wildlife in the ranch country where he lived. Wherever he went, he always saw deer, elk, and antelope and, like a few weeks ago, even bears.

When they got to town, Parker's dad drove to the field next to the rodeo grounds and parked the truck. They unloaded their horses and rode to the south side of town where the floats, bands, and horseback riders were congregating for the parade. Parker just knew everybody was looking at his new saddle.

He started looking for Joe Dan and soon found him talking to some of the kids in their class who they hadn't seen since summer vacation started. He rode over and said hello to everyone.

As usual, Joe Dan was riding Centavo and the two boys

sat their horses as they talked to their friends. When they heard the parade coordinator blow her whistle signaling everyone to line up, they said goodbye and took their places among the other parade participants.

Parker saw his dad at the front with the New Mexico state flag in his right hand. His Dad got to carry the flag as an honor because he was the vice-president of the association that put on the rodeo. Parker was proud of him and the way he sat his horse at the front of the parade.

Soon the parade coordinator rode along the line and made the final inspection of the riders, floats, bands, fire trucks, police cars, and kids on bicycles. Once she'd ridden back to the front of the line she turned and yelled, "All right, people, let's look sharp now," and the parade was on.

Chester caught the excitement and held his head high as he moved out. Parker knew he liked being in front of the people because he acted that way only on rodeo day. About half way along the route, Parker saw Sidney Allen, who he thought was the prettiest girl in school. She smiled and waved at him. He shyly waved back, hoping Joe Dan didn't see. Sidney wore a light blue shirt that matched her blue eyes, and her blond hair was tied in a ponytail.

When the procession reached the rodeo grounds, the riders rode through the gate, and Parker and Joe Dan loped their horses over to the truck. They loosened their cinches, and got a drink from the water jug that Parker's dad kept behind the seat. Even though it was only 9:30 am, it was starting to get hot. And as usually happened at this time of year, a few clouds were starting to build over the mountains to the west of town.

The boys tightened their cinches, got back on, and rode to the roping chutes. Donnie Jeffers had just finished warming up his grey horse and was sitting on him next to the arena fence. Parker and Joe Dan rode up beside him and reached across their horses to shake hands.

Donnie was their hero. He was friendly with everyone, but Parker and Joe Dan were his favorites. He never forgot them at Christmas time or at their birthdays, when he unfailingly gave them either pocketknives or buckskin gloves as presents. He was almost thirty years old and not married, although most of the girls in town and on the ranches wanted him as a boyfriend. But like he told the boys one time, he liked them all and wasn't ready to give too much time to just one.

"What're you cowboys spending your money on today?" Donnie asked.

"We're going to rope calves and run in the cowpony race," Joe Dan said.

"Well that's a good way to spend the Fourth of July," Donnie replied. Then he noticed Parker's saddle.

"Lordy, Lordy, Lordy. Where d'ya get that wood, son?

Parker smiled wide and said, "Mr. Oliver made it. It's my birthday present, and this is the first day I've ever forked it."

"Well, there ain't no better day to be sporting a new riggin'", Donnie said. "Specially, if'n you've got more than cowpunchers to admire it, if you know what I mean."

Parker got a sheepish grin and Joe Dan piped up, "Oh, don't worry about him. Sidney Allen's already been scopin' him out, even though I don't think she cares much about saddles."

"Well, sure she does. Why else would she be lookin' at your compadre there?" Donnie asked with a grin.

Parker reined away from the arena, wanting out of the discussion. Joe Dan and Donnie called to him, but he kept riding like he didn't hear them.

"Wonder why he rode off like that? Ya think we hit on something a little too close?" Donnie asked, again with a grin.

"Well, I don't know, but I better go follow him and make sure he keeps his mind on his business," Joe Dan said and he rode off after his friend.

He found Parker talking to his dad. As he rode up, Parker said, "My Dad's already entered you."

Joe Dan stepped off his horse and said, "Well, thanks," and started to reach for the money in his pocket.

Tom said, "Don't worry about it, son. I took care of it. As much as you help us on the ranch, it's the least I can do. And I really appreciated your help the other day when I busted my head in the pasture. You guys just have a good time."

"Well, gosh. You didn't have to do that. You know I like helping any time I can," Joe Dan said and shook the older man's hand.

The boys stepped on their horses and rode to the arena. People were everywhere, either warming up their horses or sitting on them talking and laughing. Kids ran back and forth clutching cotton candy or bottles of pop. The excitement was electric.

Parker and Joe Dan caught the excitement, too. Joe Dan said, "By gosh, the nearest thing to heaven has to be the 4th of July in Spanish Fork."

"You said it," his friend replied, and they spurred their horses into a lope.

As they got to the arena, the first saddle bronc rider came out of the chute. His horse took a big jump once he cleared the gate and then bucked from side to side as he went across the arena. But the cowboy spurred him every jump and even fanned him with his hat to make him buck harder. When the whistle blew, he kicked out of his stirrups and landed on his feet. He waved his hat to the crowd.

The boys clapped with the rest of the crowd. "Who's that?" Parker asked. "I've never seen him before, but he's pretty darn salty, isn't he?"

"You bet he is," Joe Dan said. "I heard Donnie talking about him the other day. He just hired on to the Double Us. Said he was a pretty good hand, but he didn't say anything about him being able to ride saddle broncs like that."

Sitting on their horses the boys watched the rest of the saddle bronc riding and then rode to the back side of the arena where Donnie was again warming up his horse.

"You want to bet Donnie wins the calf roping?" Parker asked. "I'll bet you a Coke and a candy bar."

"Yeah, I bet you would," Joe Dan said. "That'd be the easiest bet you ever won. I think I'll just wait for a wager that might be a little more interesting."

Donnie finished his warm up and headed to the roping chute. Two girls on horseback tried to get him stop to talk before he got there, but he just waved as he rode past them and kept on his way.

"Now that's a man that keeps his mind on his business. Not like some people I know," Joe Dan said with a grin.

"Would you cut it out? You're just talking big because Lacey isn't here," Parker replied.

"Well that might be true, but I ain't gonna deny it like some people I know," Joe Dan said.

Parker shook his head at his friend's teasing and led the way to the arena where they found a spot where they could watch. The first two ropers caught their calves with good times, but the next two missed. The fifth roper caught and tied his calf quicker than the first two. The announcer reported that his time was eight and a half seconds, which was two seconds faster than the first two ropers. The announcer yelled to him to wave to the crowd being that he was leading the event. The cowboy responded with a wave of his hat, and the crowd applauded their congratulations.

Donnie was next to rope. He backed his grey horse into the box and swung his rope over his head a few times. His horse stood poised with his ears forward ready to pounce after the calf when it left the chute.

He nodded that he was ready and the chute gate flew open. The calf dashed out, and Donnie's horse charged in behind. Donnie swung twice and let his loop fly. It caught the calf neatly around the neck, and Donnie pulled his slack and slid his horse to a stop. He sprung off on the left side and ran down the rope.

After he flanked the calf, he dropped the loop of his pigging string over its left front leg and then grabbed both hind legs. He wrapped all three two times with the string, tied them with a half-hitch, and then threw his hands in the air.

The boys smiled at each other and yelled for their friend. They knew he had a fast time, but then they noticed a commotion at the chute. The judge there was shaking his head and holding up his right hand indicating that Donnie's horse had broken the barrier rope that ensured the calf got a fair start.

"Ah, tough luck, cowboy," the announcer said. "Folks, the chute judge says Donnie's horse came out of the box before the calf got his start, so we're going to have add five seconds to his time. And that's a shame, because he ran a 5.9. So now all he's going to get is your applause."

Donnie shrugged his shoulders, but waved to the crowd as he walked back to his horse. His misfortune didn't seem to bother the girls he'd seen earlier because they met him on their horses at the arena gate. He didn't seem to be too bothered either, because he smiled at them, and they all rode off to where his horse trailer was parked.

The boys wanted to talk to him, but they decided he had enough company right then, so they decided to find Parker's mom and have lunch.

10

COW PONY RACE

They found her sitting on a lawn chair on the south side of the arena where Tom had set the blue tarp up for her. It was cool under it, especially when a breeze blew through. The boys slid off their horses and tied them to the horse trailer. When they got to the tarp, they flopped down on the grass by their bedrolls.

Parker's mother smiled at them and said, "I wondered if you boys were ever going to get hungry." Interesting, Parker thought, his mom's hair was in a pony tail just like Sidney's, and she was wearing a blue shirt too. What a coincidence. No matter, he still thought she was sure pretty for a mom.

"We've been hungry a long time, but we wanted to be over where we could see Donnie rope," Parker said. "He had bad luck, huh?"

"Yes, he did, but I bet he'll get over it pretty quick with the help of those two girls from the Draggin' S that were waiting for him at the gate. They looked like they were ready to give him all the encouragement and support he was going to need," said his mother with a grin

The boys smiled back, and Parker walked to the cooler and pulled out two bottles of Coke. They dripped with ice and cold water. He opened them with the opener that hung from a string on the side of the box. He handed one to Joe Dan, and then took a long drink out of his bottle.

"Well, boys, you know there aren't any surprises for 4th of July lunch. We've got fried chicken, potato salad, pork and beans, and pickles. Make your plates whenever you want. Your Dad said he wouldn't be over until after 1:00 o'clock because he had to help set up the barrels for the barrel race," Parker's mother said.

She handed them paper plates and forks, and then started opening the containers that held the food. They filled their plates with everything and each selected a drumstick and a thigh.

When they sat down, Parker's mother handed them each a napkin. "I know we're eating at a rodeo arena, but I still want you to use napkins," she said. "And you boys could try eating some white meat every once in a while, you know. You might even like it."

Parker and Joe Dan nodded at each other, and Parker said, "Ah, Mom, we know it's good, but we wouldn't want to eat it all up so that you and Dad couldn't have any."

"Well, that's so thoughtful of you young men," she replied with a smile. "You're always thinking about everybody else but yourselves."

The boys grinned at each other, but dropped their heads and continued to eat, knowing it was best not to continue the discussion. They were cleaning their plates when they heard the backfire of a vehicle out in the arena. They jumped to their feet and climbed the fence to see what was going on.

On the far side of the arena in front of the grandstand they saw Travis Taylor, the rodeo clown, bent under the hood of a beat up yellow Volkswagon, banging on various parts of the engine with a rubber hammer. After a while he stood up and yelled something to the rodeo announcer that the boys couldn't hear.

"What's wrong with your car, Travis?" the announcer asked.

The rodeo clown answered something back and the announcer said, "You don't know. Well, do ya really think that beatin' on it with a hammer is the way to fix it?"

The clown answered back, and the announcer said, "Oh, so you're a mechanic, are you. I don't think I'm gonna bother asking you where you went to school."

Travis went back under the hood but soon backed out and slammed it shut. He got in behind the steering wheel and turned the key. Nothing happened at first, until suddenly the hood flew open and an explosion of fireworks shot out from the engine.

Travis fell out of the door turning a somersault in the process. He jumped up, ran to the trunk and grabbed an oversized fire extinguisher, muttering all the while to the announcer that he had everything under control.

Once in front of the car he started spraying the extinguisher on the engine which ignited into flames. The shock of the fire propelled Travis on his back, and the announcer said, "Son, I know you're qualified but I think if you do too much more mechanicin', you're gonna get yourself hurt."

Travis stood up and nodded his head in agreement. He motioned to the announcer to wait a second and then ran to the side gate of the arena and soon returned with two harnessed Shetland ponies. He drove them to the front of the car and hitched the traces to the bumper.

He shut the hood and with the lines in his right hand, he climbed on top of the car. Saying something to the announcer, he clucked to the ponies and they started pulling the car out of the arena.

"Folks, ol' Travis says not to worry. He's got all the horse power he needs," the announcer said. "Let's hear it for him." The crowd cheered as the clown made his way out of the arena.

"Next up, we're gonna have the wild cow milking. You teams that are entered meet the judge over at the bucking chutes. And then those of you that are gonna be in the cow pony race, you better get your horses warmed up because we're gonna race right after," the announcer said.

Parker and Joe Dan stepped off the fence and put their paper plates and Coke bottles in the plastic trash sack that Parker's mother had hung off of the tailgate of the pickup.

"Well, amigo, you better get your bronco ready," Joe Dan said to Parker.

"I was just thinking the same thing," Parker replied and walked to his mother and hugged her.

"Now you be careful," she said.

"Oh Mom, don't worry. I've done this before," Parker said patting her shoulder.

"Yeah, I know. But I still want you to be careful," she said.

The boys walked to their horses and mounted. When they rode behind the horse trailers next to the open field, they saw Donnie on his grey horse riding toward them. There was a pretty girl with long brown hair riding next to him, but she wasn't one of the two from the Draggin' S.

When they met, Joe Dan said to Donnie, "That was bad luck about the barrier."

"Well, yeah, but it ain't the first time ol' Cisco's left the box a little too early. We'll get 'em next time," Donnie said. "Say, I want to you boys to meet Laurie Hill. She's from Amarillo."

The boys tipped their hats and introduced themselves to the girl. She smiled at them, which caused Joe Dan to get shy and hang his head so he wouldn't have to make eye contact with her. Donnie and Laurie smiled at each other, and Donnie said, "You boys about to race those horses of yours?"

Joe Dan got up enough nerve to look up and say, "Naw,

I'm not. Centavo's too old to be racing. Besides I'd hate to win the thing and show up my compadre here."

"Yeah, I bet you'd really have to worry about that," Parker said as he playfully pushed Joe Dan in the shoulder. "If I didn't like that old plug of yours so much, I'd tell you just what I thought of him."

"Well, any way, good luck, amigo," Donnie said to Parker. You're gonna need it with everybody I've heard's gonna be in it.

"Thanks, I know it's gonna be pretty tough," Parker said.

He paused for a second and then said, "Well, I guess I'd better get warmed up. I'll see ya'll later. It was nice to meet you, Laurie" he said with a smile.

He waved to them over his shoulder as he kicked into a lope. Once he was out in the middle of the field, he rode Chester in big figure eight patterns until he felt the horse was loose enough. He turned back to where Donnie, Laurie, and Joe Dan had been, and seeing that his friend was sitting on his horse by himself, motioned to him to follow him to the north side of the arena where the race would start.

Once the boys were together, Joe Dan asked, "Well, how d'ya think he's feeling."

"Seems pretty good. I just hope I can hold him down at the first so that he doesn't give out before the end of the race. You know how excited he gets when he gets in a race," Parker said. "All I know is that I sure like this saddle, and even if we don't win, we're going to look good."

Before long the announcer said over the loud speaker that the cow pony race would be the next event and that everybody entered should check in with the judge who had just ridden onto the track that surrounded the arena. Parker reined Chester onto the track and headed for the judge, who was wearing a white shirt and red bandana sitting on his horse about a hundred yards away. Other riders, his competitors, were doing the same and by the time they reached the judge, Parker counted eleven in all.

"This could be a little tricky with all these horses," he muttered to himself.

The judge smiled at the riders and held up his hand and asked for quiet. "First of all, I want you all to be careful going around this track. It's in pretty good shape, but when I rode it this morning I found a few holes that could give you some trouble if you're not paying attention."

"I know you're all friends, but I want to remind you to give each other plenty of room and don't run over each other. Take care of yourselves and your horses. Now, line up in front of the grandstand, and we'll get started."

He rode to a chalk line that had been drawn across the track in the middle of the grandstand. The racers followed. Parker rode with Kelly Johnson and Chris Davis, friends from school who lived in town and had horses.

"Kelly, you really think that mare of yours is going to be able to keep up," Chris joked good-naturedly.

"You just better make sure you don't get beat by a girl."

When they got to the starting line, Parker stopped on Kelly's left and Chris pulled in on her right. They were on the outside of the line of racers meaning they would have farther to run.

"I'm glad the judge put me on the outside so that the rest of you'd have a chance," Chris said nonchalantly.

"Oh be quiet, you wind bag. You better think more about your ridin' than your talkin,'" Kelly told him, and they focused their attention on the judge and the start of the race.

The judge rode to the inside rail and turned his horse to the racers. Satisfied that they were in a straight line, he raised his flag and said, "Okay, everybody ready. On your mark, get set, go!"

The riders shot ahead in a mass, each spurring their horse as they tried to get the lead. Before they reached the end of the grandstand, the bay horse in the third position had gotten a ten-yard lead, and his rider was quirting him for all he was worth.

The rest of the riders trailed in behind, each jockeying for a position as they came around the first turn. Kelly and Parker were neck and neck in the middle, but Chris had dropped back to last.

By the time the bay horse got to the back stretch, his lead had shrunk to five yards, and he was weakening. Three riders were gaining on him, two of them being Kelly and Parker. Chester was running well, but when they hit the far turn, Parker wasn't sure if his horse was going to be able to maintain his pace.

Kelly's mare, Senorita, stretched out and picked up speed when she came to the last turn in front of the grandstand. Kelly leaned low on her neck and her long brown hair trailed from behind her black hat. Parker noticed her hair because she passed him with two hundred yards left in the race, and then passed the bay horse with a hundred yards left to go. When she crossed the finish line, she was twenty yards in the lead.

As she pulled Senorita to a stop, she turned and waved to the crowd who was cheering wildly for her. Parker rode up and shook her hand.

"Dang, I knew Senorita was fast, but I never knew she was that fast," Parker said.

"Well, there's some things girls just don't tell," Kelly said with a smile. They rode together to where the judge sat on his horse. He smiled at her and said, "That was some ridin', missy. Ya wanna sell that mare?"

"No, I don't believe so. I think she'd get lonesome if she didn't have me bringing her oats," Kelly replied.

"Well, you're probably right. Anyway, I'm proud of you. What're you gonna do with all that prize money?" he asked.

"I don't know just yet, but I bet it'll be something for her. She's the one who earned it."

Right then, Chris rode up. His head hung a little sheepishly, but Kelly smiled at him and said, "Don't worry about it, Chris. You just had bad luck."

"Oh, you're just being nice. I knew ol' Dollar couldn't win. I was just playin' with ya'll."

They shook hands with the judge and turned their horses to ride off the track. "Just a minute, Kelly," the announcer said over the loud speaker. "The arena director wants you to meet him out in the arena so he can give you your buckle." Kelly turned up to look at him in the crow's nest and waved and then reined toward the arena gate.

When she loped to the center of the arena, the grandstand erupted in applause. "Look at that girl, ladies and gentlemen. She sure showed those cowboys how to ride, didn't she? Let's hear it for her," the announcer said over the loud speaker.

Kelly waved to thank the crowd and then slid Senorita to a stop in front of Tobe Jenkins, the arena director, who was horseback across from the bucking chutes. He had her buckle in his hand, and when she stopped, he shook hands with her.

"I don't think the Comanches ever rode as good as you," he said as he smiled and gave her the buckle.

"Well, thanks, but Senorita gets the credit. I just hung on," Kelly said with a grin. She turned and rode out of the arena looking for Parker. She couldn't wait to show him what she'd won.

11

WILD HORSE RACE

After the race, Parker rode to the roping chutes. He located the roping judge and found out from him that he and Kelly would go third in the ribbon roping that was scheduled after the wild horse race. Parker decided to ride Chester to the south side of the chutes so he could get a good view of the action, which next to the roping events was his favorite.

Kelly found him there. She eased Senorita next to him and with a big smile said, "Look what they gave me."

Even though Parker was disappointed he hadn't done better in the race, he couldn't help being happy for Kelly. She was a nice girl, and he'd always liked her. Besides, she was real pretty.

Parker took the buckle from her and said, "Wow, that's something. They sure give out a lot better buckles than they did when we ran barrels as kids, don't they?"

"Yeah, they do. Now I'm going to have to see if my Dad will let me get a new belt from Mr. Oliver to put it on. It wouldn't do to wear it with one of my old ones," she said.

"Well, if I know anything about it, I bet your Dad will look at it about the same way. I don't ever remember him denying you much of anything," Parker said with a grin.

"You might be right about that. I've really never thought about it," she replied with her own sly grin.

"Well, if I rope well enough in the ribbon roping maybe you'll get another buckle to add to your collection," Parker said.

"I wouldn't mind that," Kelly said she took back her buckle.

Over the public address system, they heard the announcer say, "You boys entered in the wild horse race get out in the arena as fast as you can. The judges want to talk to you. Your horses are ready in the chutes."

From all sides of the arena, cowboys started climbing over and through the fence, pulling down their hats and hurrying as fast as they could, some with their saddles thrown over their shoulders. Once they were gathered around the judges, Parker counted almost twenty of them. Looking at the bucking chutes, he counted six broncs loaded in the chutes, so he figured there must be eighteen cowboys, three to a team.

After the cowboys got their instructions, they separated into teams and started to the chutes. A man from each team went to their assigned chute and took the lead rope of the horse inside. Several of the horses kicked and reared when they felt the pressure of the halters on their noses.

Parker looked at Kelly and said with a smile, "I'm tellin' ya, those cowboys are gonna have fun." She nodded with a laugh.

When they looked back, they saw one of the judges drop his flag, and the chute gates flew open all at the same time. Two of the broncs stampeded past the cowboys who held their ropes. One of them couldn't hold on, and as he sprawled on all fours in the dirt, he watched his horse buck to the far side of the arena.

The other cowboy held on, although his horse ran so fast that he couldn't keep up and soon lost his feet. The horse dragged him until his teammates caught up with him and grabbed the rope.

When the horse felt the additional pressure of the rope on his nose, he wheeled and set back on his hind feet. One of the cowboys then let go of the rope and ran back to get his saddle. By the time he returned, one of the other men had gingerly walked up the rope and grabbed the horse's left ear, twisting it hard to distract its attention.

The cowboy with the saddle then walked slowly beside him, and, when he got to the horse's shoulder, started to lift the saddle onto the horse's back. As he did, the horse struck the saddle with his left hind foot and knocked it out of his hand. The motion caused the man holding the horse's ear to also lose his grip, and the horse backed away, dragging the cowboy holding the rope as he went.

In the meantime, three other teams had gotten to a similar stage. The team nearest Parker and Kelly was the first to get their horse saddled. When they had cinched the saddle as tight as they could, two of them grabbed onto the horse's ear, while the third took the lead rope in his left hand, put his boot in the left stirrup, grabbed the horn, and pulled into the saddle. When he had his right foot in the stirrup, he nodded to his partners, and they let the horse go.

The horse froze for a few seconds, and then, realizing he had a rider on his back, dropped his head and started bucking across the arena floor. Each time he hit the ground, he let out a tremendous squall that could be heard all over the arena. For all of the noise he made, however, he didn't buck very hard, and the cowboy rode him easily. As the horse bucked along, the cowboy did his best to guide him toward the painted red, white, and blue barrel that sat near the fence in front of the grandstands.

On the other side of the arena, another rider had mounted. His horse jumped twice and then stampeded toward the grandstand fence. The cowboy tried to pull him up, but having no luck, held on until the horse struck the fence, running at full speed. The cowboy sailed over his saddle, onto the horse's neck, and then over the fence. He landed squarely on his back.

He didn't move for a few seconds. Before anyone could get to him, though, he sat up, took off his hat, and shook his head. He appeared dazed, but when Travis jumped the fence to check on him, he looked up, said something, and then stood up. Before he started to walk to the fence on wobbly feet, he turned to the grandstand and waved his hat to let the fans know he was all right.

By this time the cowboy on the first horse had his horse bucking toward the painted barrel. The horse had accelerated and was bucking harder, although the cowboy was still riding him okay. He had lost his right stirrup but had his spur dug into the cinch so he was keeping his seat.

Only two other cowboys had gotten mounted, but they both got bucked off within the first few jumps. Seeing that he was the only one horseback, the cowboy took off his hat and starting fanning his bronc, which for the moment caused the horse to buck harder. Before the horse reached the barrel, though, he slowed down, stopped bawling, and was barely crow-hopping when he passed the judge sitting on top of the barrel who dropped his flag signifying that he'd won the race.

The crowd cheered. It looked liked the cowboy was going to keep riding the horse, but as he raised his hat to wave to the fans, the horse made a sideways jump to the left and dumped the cowboy face down onto the arena floor. The cheers turned to laughs, but the cowboy jumped up and kicked dirt in the direction of the bucking horse.

"That's one of the best wild horse races I've ever seen on the 4th," Parker said to Kelly. "I'd like to get in it someday. I wouldn't mind winning a wild horse race buckle, especially if it was from Spanish Fork."

"Well, until that happens, you just worry about catching your calf and maybe we'll get a buckle together today. What d'ya say we go get a Coke before you rope."

12

RIBBON ROPING

"Well, I'm gonna go warm up Chester again," Parker said to Kelly after they finished their Cokes. "What're you gonna run in?"

"Oh, I brought tennis shoes. I'm afraid I'd trip too many times if I tried to run in my boots," she replied.

"Okay, I'll see you in a minute," Parker said as he turned toward where the trailers were parked. He slow loped Chester in a few figure eight patterns but took it easy because his horse didn't need much after the race he'd just been in. When he was satisfied that Chester was ready, he took his rope from the swell of his saddle and put the horn knot over the saddle horn and pulled it tight. He built a loop and as he pointed Chester back to the arena, he swung the loop over his head a few times and then threw a few practice loops on the ground.

"Feeling pretty good today," he said to himself. "Chester, my boy, all you have to do is put me there, and I'll do the rest," as he rubbed his horse's neck.

He rode to the roping chutes and found Joe Dan, who

was sitting on his horse next to the fence. "Who's going to win this beside you or me?" he asked with a grin.

"I don't rightly know but the way I look at it, I won't mind making a donation of my entry fee to the association if I don't draw a check. It's pretty cheap entertainment if you ask me," Joe Dan replied.

"I'm with you, compadre."

They looked toward the crow's nest when the announcer starting naming the contestants and their order for the ribbon roping.

"First up, we've got a La Cueva Ranch cowboy, Darren Sanchez. Then we've got Joel Saunders on deck followed by Parker Smith of the Box S in the hole.

"Good luck, buddy," Joe Dan said.

"Thanks," Parker replied, "but like they say, I'd rather be good than lucky."

"Oh, you'll do okay. Just keep your eye on the ball, or whatever it is you're doing," Joe Dan said with a grin.

The first calf was run into the roping chute while Darren Sanchez rode his horse into the box on the right side. He backed into the corner, took a few practice swings, and nodded for the calf.

When the calf saw the chute gate open, he shot out in a frightened effort to escape. Darren slipped in behind him and took three swings before he threw his rope. The loop settled neatly over the calf's neck and Darren pulled the slack. As the rope stretched and slowed the calf, Darren dropped from his saddle and ran toward the calf with his hand on the rope. When he reached the calf it was facing him on the end of the rope, and he grabbed it by the front right leg and then over the left shoulder to keep it as still as he could. As he did so, a girl in a bright pink shirt and pig tails ran in from the right hand side and reached for the red ribbon that was tied to the calf's tail. Missing it at first, she got it on the second try. She turned and sprinted toward the chutes where the arena judge stood with an upraised flag.

In her hurry she tripped and fell to her knees after ten yards, but scrambled to her feet and continued on her way. When she got to the chute, she tripped again just as the judge dropped the flag. Several cowboys who were near went to help her, but before they got to her, she was up smiling and waving to the crowd.

"That's Daisy Aragon, folks," the announcer said from the crow's nest. "Now, I tell you, that girl can run. Darren and Daisy will get a time of 18.46 seconds. Let's hear it for them."

The crowd cheered. The next roper rode into the box but missed his calf when it ducked to the left as it dashed from the chute. "Tough luck, cowboy. But, we'll have to see you next year," the announcer said. "Next up, we've got Parker Smith from the Box S, and Kelly Johnson, who won the cow pony race, is going to run for him

As Parker walked Chester through the gate into the roping box, he looked to the right side of the arena and saw Kelly crawl through the fence to get into position for her run to the calf if he roped it.

"You know, she is pretty," he said to himself as he watched her talking to a girl beside her. She had changed into a dark green shirt and was wearing the black hat that set off her summer tan. "I wonder why I'm just noticing." Then, after a second's thought, he said, "Geez, I guess I better pay attention to my business if I want to try to win this."

He backed Chester into the corner of the box and lifted the horse's head with his reins so that he could see the calf in the chute. He took a few practice swings and sat down in his saddle as deeply as he could. When he saw that Chester was ready, he nodded to the cowboy sitting on the chute who released the gate.

The calf shot forward. Without being spurred, Chester lunged after him and before they were fifteen yards down the arena, Parker threw his loop. When he saw that he was going to catch, he pulled the slack out of the rope and drew on his reins to slow Chester. They stopped the calf within five yards, and Parker flung from the saddle and started down the rope.

Initially, the calf tried to get away, but with the aid of the rope Parker held him long enough so that he could grab a front leg. Before he had the calf completely stopped, he saw Kelly come in and grab the ribbon. She smiled at Parker before she turned toward the chute and ran like she was trying to steal second base.

The people in the stands and along the arena fence cheered. Their encouragement seemed to make her run faster and her dark brown hair streamed from her hat as she raced for the judge. Within what seemed like only seconds she flew past him, and he threw his flag.

The crowd erupted. Parker pumped his fist as he trotted back to his horse. The announcer shouted, "Ladies and gentlemen, we've got new leaders. Parker and Kelly's time is 16.17 seconds. I knew Kelly had a fast horse, but I didn't know she was just about as fast.

Parker got back on Chester and patted him on the neck. As he coiled his rope, he trotted back to the chute where several of the cowboys were shaking Kelly's hand. He rode up beside her, smiled, and stuck out his hand. She reached for it and pulled herself up behind him in the saddle.

They rode together across the arena to the gate by the bucking chutes where one of the arena judges let them out. Parker noticed that Kelly wasn't saying much, but was holding on to him a little more than she probably needed to. And he admitted that he didn't mind.

He reined Chester toward the blue tarp so they could talk to his mother. She got out of her lawn chair when she saw them riding up and waved. "Good for both of you. Even if you don't win, you're the best looking couple out there," she said with a smile.

Parker knew that his mother's comment made him blush, but he said, "Did you see ol' Chester? He was on that calf like a mongoose."

"Yes, he was. He's a good boy," his mother said as she stroked the horse's neck. "You kids can be proud of yourselves. That was a great run."

Parker helped Kelly slide off. "Gosh, I don't know if I can stand to watch those other teams. I really want to win this," she said.

"Oh, come on. It's just a roping, and besides you've already got a pretty nice buckle," Parker said.

"Yeah, but like I told you, I want another one. Tie up your horse, and let's go watch the rest of them."

They said goodbye to Parker's mother and trotted back to the roping chute. Another team had already gone with a time three seconds longer than theirs. They found an open spot on the fence and climbed up.

Parker turned to Kelly, "I know I roped pretty well, but, if we win this, it's going to be because of how fast you ran."

"Well, I just tried as hard as I could. You know I don't know any other way," she said.

"Yeah, I know," Parker said with a grin.

As they watched the next contestant move into the box, Joe Dan came up behind them on his horse. "Hey, I've got a problem. Lacey was going to run for me, but she just came up and said she can't because she's got to go help her dad back at the store. I guess there're so many people in town wanting to buy hats and boots that he's swamped. I asked her if she couldn't wait until I roped but she said her dad said to come right now. I don't know what to do."

Parker and Kelly looked at each other and nodded. "Well,

I don't know if you'd want me, but I'll run for you," Kelly said. "You know I'm no track star like Lacey."

Joe Dan face broke into a smile. "Would you? Boy, I'd appreciate it. I didn't want to go home without getting to rope."

"Yeah, but what if she runs faster for you than me?" Parker asked with a grin.

"Oh don't worry, amigo. I probably won't even catch. Besides, if I win, I'll let you wear my buckle any time you want," laughed his friend as he turned his horse toward the chutes.

After Kelly jumped off the fence into the arena, she looked up at Parker and said, "Well, maybe between the two of you I'll get another buckle after all."

"Oh, Kelly. You ought to be more like us. We're just in it for sport."

"Sure you are. Not a competitive bone in either of you, is there?"

"Well, maybe a few," Parker said grinning. "But, I sure would hate it if you fell down or something trying to help my buddy win a buckle."

"Yeah, I bet you would. I'll see you in a minute after I do some work for your best friend. It shouldn't take long," she said as she turned to take her position along the fence.

Pretty spunky, Parker thought, as he watched her walk away.

Joe Dan was the last roper. When it was his turn, the announcer said, "Folks, Parker Smith is still in first place, but now his best friend, Joe Dan Peters is up. And, how about this? Kelly Johnson, who ran for Parker, is going to run for Joe Dan. It looks like they're trying to keep it all in the family."

The crowd clapped as Joe Dan rode Centavo into the back of the roping box. When they were ready, Joe Dan called for the calf, and it shot out in a straight line as Joe Dan reined in behind it. Centavo's head was low and his ears pinned back as he put Joe Dan into position.

Joe Dan swung twice and threw his loop neatly over the calf's head. He pulled his slack and brought Centavo to a quick stop. By the time he got off and ran to the calf, Kelly was already there. She stripped the ribbon from the calf's tail and before Joe Dan realized it, she was on her way to the chutes.

"Now, come on folks! Let's help her along," the announcer shouted.

Puffs of dust followed her as she ran across the arena, and when she passed the judge, her hat fell off. After she caught her breath, she stood smiling as the cowboys around congratulated her.

The smile on Joe Dan's face was just as wide. He coiled his rope and got on his horse. As he rode back to the chutes, the announcer said, "Well, ladies and gentlemen, they did it. "Their time is 15.97 which makes them not only the leaders, but the winners of this year's ribbon roping. That's pretty darn good. Let's hear it for them."

Before Joe Dan got to the chutes, Parker ran in from the side. He reached up and shook his friend's hand and said, "By gosh, you beat me fair and square. That was some roping. I got to tell you, I'm proud of you."

"I appreciate it. You know, everybody gets lucky sometime. But to tell you the truth, Kelly's the one that won it," Joe Dan said as he watched Kelly walk toward them.

She was still smiling. She approached Parker and surprised him with a hug and a kiss on the cheek. "Sorry, cowboy, but now I guess I've got to ask my dad if he'll buy me two belts."

"I still don't think you've got a problem," Parker said as he helped her get up behind Joe Dan. "I tell you what. I want to buy you winners a cherry lime Coke and as many burritos as you can eat."

"That sounds good to me," Joe Dan said. "Winning sure makes a man hungry," he said as he winked at his best friend.

They walked out of the arena. After they had eaten, they

got back on the arena fence and watched the bull riding which was the last event of the day. Neither Parker nor Joe Dan cared for bull riding because it wasn't a ranch cowboy event, but they always watched because some of their friends were usually entered.

Before the event was over, Kelly said, "Well, cowboys, I think I'm going to go get Senorita and head home. I'm a little tired."

"Well, you ought to be after all you did today. "Thanks for what you did," Joe Dan said as she hugged him goodbye.

"No reason to thank me. We wouldn't have gotten anything if you hadn't roped like you did," she replied.

"Well, I don't know. I tell you what, why don't we just thank Centavo. He did the hard part," Joe Dan said.

"There you go. Be sure to give him some extra oats before you turn him out tonight," Kelly said as she trotted off to get her horse.

Both boys watched her as she left. "You know, I guess I never realized how nice she is," Parker said.

"You better watch yourself, compadre. I don't think a certain Sidney Allen is going to appreciate you mooning over another girl."

"Oh, I just like Kelly as a friend. Besides, I'm too busy being a scholar to worry about girls."

"Son, are you forgetting who you're talking to? To hear you talk, you'll be wanting to study your school books tonight instead of going to the dance. Or maybe you'll just study in between dances," Joe Dan said as he jabbed his friend in the ribs.

"Well, I don't know. I guess it just depends on who shows up," Parker said with a grin. "Come on, let's go help my mom get packed up so we can go home."

13

SWIMMING

On Saturday two weeks after the rodeo, Parker's mother and dad left at 6:30 in the morning for their monthly trip to town to buy groceries and horse feed. Normally, Parker would have gone with them, but July had really been hot, and he and Joe Dan had planned all week to go swimming.

With his parents gone and no cow work to do, Parker stayed in bed longer than usual. He was in a deep sleep when Josie jumped on the bed and starting licking his face. Not only did she want to go outside, she didn't understand why Parker was still laying in bed when the sun was shining.

Parker smiled and stroked her head. He got out of bed and walked her to the back door, taking time to get her a dog treat out of the pantry as he walked by. Back in his room, he pulled on his favorite summer shirt, a faded red one with the sleeves cut off.

Like all cowboys, he usually wore long sleeve shirts, but he had this old one to wear in the summer when he wasn't working. It was a lot cooler. After he pulled on his boots, he got his bathing suit from the chest of drawers and walked to the kitchen to make some baloney sandwiches for Joe Dan and him. He made five of them in all, four with mustard and one without. The one without mustard had an extra piece of baloney. It was for Josie.

He put the sandwiches in paper sacks and then got some apples from the refrigerator. He walked out the back door and walked to the corrals to saddle Chester. By the time he had the horse in and fed, he heard Josie bark outside the saddle house. He knew she must have seen Joe Dan.

He walked outside and saw his friend jogging up on his bay horse, Centavo. When Joe Dan pulled to a stop, he jumped off and waited for Josie to come to him to get petted. Besides Parker, Joe Dan was her favorite. Joe Dan hugged her, and while he told her she was she was a good girl, he pulled a dog biscuit from his Levi jacket and watched her wag her tail as she crunched it.

Parker opened the corral gate and walked out with Chester. He smiled at his friend as he handed him one of the sandwich sacks. After Joe Dan rolled his lunch in his yellow slicker, they mounted their horses and rode west toward the mouth of Manuelas Canyon.

It was a beautiful morning. Meadowlarks sang on both sides of them and every once in a while, Josie decided she needed to chase one of them. The boys breathed in the pungent scent of the prairie grass and sage that was all the more fragrant because of the rain that had fallen two days before.

It took them more than an hour to reach the mouth of the canyon. When they got there, they crossed the creek and started up the west side that was dotted with piñon and juniper trees. The sun beat down on them as they trotted along, and they smelled the sweat of their horses mixed with the scent of the trees.

By the time they got to the swimming hole they were

hot. They quickly pulled the saddles off their horses, and Joe Dan led Centavo to a grassy place behind some cottonwood trees so that he could graze while they swam. After he hobbled the horse, Joe Dan ran back to the edge of the creek and was surprised to see that Parker had already put his swimming suit on and had ridden Chester out into the deepest part of the pool.

He quickly pulled his swimming suit from inside his slicker and changed into it. He scrambled up the side of the rock ledge that hung over the pool and looked down at his friend who had just jumped off of Chester. The horse was standing patiently in the middle of the pool so that Parker could jump off his back.

When the boys went swimming with Chester, they liked to make believe they were Comanche Indians and fall off his back as if they had been shot by cavalry soldiers. Other times, they pretended they were circus performers and tried to execute flips and rolls like they'd seen at the circus that had come to town last summer.

Even though it was July, the water was cold and after thirty minutes the boys both crawled on Chester's back and walked him out of the creek. When they got to the bank, Joe Dan slid off and handed Parker his boots. Parker rode Chester over to where Centavo was grazing, pulled on his boots, and then dropped down. He took the bridle off the horse, hobbled him, and gave him a pat on the shoulder.

Chester immediately dropped his head and started grazing. Centavo took enough time to look up from where he was grazing to nicker to his partner, but soon returned to eating. Parker walked over to their saddles and picked up their slickers and ran with them to where Joe Dan was standing on a big flat rock that had heated up from the morning sun.

They unrolled the slickers and sat down on them. They took out their sandwiches and started to eat. Josie had stayed down at the creek investigating a beaver dam, but when she heard the rattling of the paper sacks, she knew it was lunch time.

She ran to the boys with a grin on her face eagerly anticipating having lunch with her boys.

Parker broke Josie's sandwich into two pieces so that she wouldn't eat it too fast. After they finished their sandwiches, the boys stretched out on their slickers and munched on the apples. Josie tried to lie down between them, but because she was wet and her hair was cold on their sides, Parker told her to lie over on the other side of the rock. With a forlorn look, she reluctantly obeyed.

Once they were warmed up, they dove back into the water and practiced their swimming strokes for as much as the small pool would allow them. Looking up at the sky, Parker estimated that it was probably about three o'clock so he yelled at Joe Dan on the other side of the pool that they better saddle their horses so that they could get home by the time his parents did.

Joe Dan waved okay and swam as fast as he could to get across the pool so he could get his horse saddled first. It was a game they always played and started several years ago when Parker's dad mentioned that he hated to be the last one saddled. They decided that they didn't like it either, primarily because it gave them another opportunity to compete with each other.

Because Parker was closer he was about to bridle his horse when Joe Dan got there. In a frantic effort Joe Dan grabbed one of Parker's saddle strings just as Parker started to throw his saddle over his horse's back. It was enough o make Parker drop the saddle on the ground.

Joe Dan quickly grabbed his bridle and put the bit in Centavo's mouth. After he brushed the horse's back off with his right hand, he reached without looking for his blanket that he'd left on top of his saddle. He was so intent on what he was doing that he hadn't notice that Parker had thrown his saddle blanket behind a nearby juniper tree.

When he didn't feel the blanket, he turned around to see

where it was. Not seeing it, he immediately turned to his friend who by this time had his saddle on his horse and was starting to cinch up. Parker did his best not to laugh, but when he felt his friend's eyes on him, he burst out laughing as he pointed to the blanket over by the tree.

"I guess that what's you get for cheatin', compadre," he said as he pulled up his cinch.

Joe Dan dropped his bridle reins, turned to his friend and said, "Well, I guess I'm just gonna have to teach you a lesson about messin' with things that don't belong to you." Without a word, he lunged at Parker and tackled him before he could step out of the way. They wrestled in the grass for a few minutes trying to pin each other, but neither had much success because they were laughing so hard. Josie barked at them and tried to get in between them.

Finally they realized they were about to roll into a cholla cactus, so they stopped, stood up, and gave each other a playful shove. "I think it'd be better if we remembered to put our clothes on the next time we start wrestling," Joe Dan said, and he walked over to pull on his Levis.

After the boys dressed, they finished saddling their horses. Parker called Josie, and they headed down the canyon. They trotted almost all the way home and didn't pull up until they got to the horse trap. Parker stepped off Chester and opened the gate. As Joe Dan rode through, he shook his friend's hand and told him he'd see him next week. Without another word, he reined Centavo toward home, waving as he went.

Parker figured Joe Dan must be as tired as he was because he said so little as he left. Usually, he would have been talking a mile a minute. "Must have been too much swimming, wrestling and sunshine for the boy," he laughed to himself as he walked to the house for supper.

14

TRIP TO TOWN

On the third day of August Parker's mother asked him if he wanted to go to town with her.

"Sure, what time are you going to go?" he asked.

"Oh, I think about nine o'clock. I've got to finish some things up in the kitchen before we go, and that'd give you time to get your chores done," she said.

"Would you mind if we went and picked up Joe Dan? I know he hasn't been to town since the Fourth of July."

"That's fine with me, but you call him ahead of time to make sure he'll be ready. I don't want to have to wait on him," his mother replied.

After Parker called Joe Dan and got his excited answer that he sure did want to go to town, Parker went to the corrals and threw the saddle horses some hay and filled up the water tank. Then he remembered his Dad had asked him to sweep the saddle house a few days before, so he got the broom out of the corner and swept it out as fast as he could. He knew that his Dad had probably noticed that he hadn't got the floor swept before now, but at least he was finally getting it done without being told a second time.

When he was done he checked to make sure Josie had water and went into the house to put on a clean shirt. Because he was going to town, he decided to change into a better pair of boots, not his best ones, but a pair that was in better shape than the ones he'd worn to do chores.

While he was pulling the second one on, he heard his mother call from outside. He ran out through the kitchen, grabbed his hat from the hook by the door and stepped out into the sunshine. He noticed it was already a lot hotter than it had been when he was doing his chores, but then what could he expect, being that it was the first week of August. He trotted to the passenger side of the pickup and reached down to pet Josie before he got in.

"Well, good boy," his mother said. "I was kinda afraid you were going to wear the same shirt you did chores in."

"Oh, Mom, you always think me and Dad are never going to dress right when we go to town," he said with a smile. "But it just so happens, we both know what we're supposed to do."

"Well, I guess," she said as she returned his smile. "But mostly I think it's just an accident when I don't have to say something."

Parker knew better than to try to defend himself, so he sat back and enjoyed the wind coming through his window as his mother drove to the Bar P headquarters. When they crossed the cattle guard into the ranch, they saw Joe Dan standing by the yard gate, fidgeting from one foot to the other.

"Well, it looks like he put on a new shirt to go to town," his mother said as Joe Dan ran up to the truck.

"Yeah, that boy's pretty much like me. Always knows how to dress," Parker said with a grin as he opened his door and got out so that Joe Dan could get in.

"Thanks for calling me," Joe Dan said as he and Parker

shook hands. "The way things were going I didn't think I was ever going to get to town before school started. And then I wouldn't mind if they forgot to take me."

"Boy, you smell nice," Parker's mother said once Joe Dan was settled in the middle. "Are you lookin' to see your girlfriend?"

"No," Joe Dan said sheepishly. "It's just that after I took a shower, I thought I ought to put on some of Dad's Old Spice after I shaved."

"Yeah, right, all you need to shave is to have the cat lick your face." Parker said as he jabbed his best friend in the ribs with his elbow. Before they were able to tussle too much, Parker's mother cautioned them by saying, "Boys," in just the right motherly tone that let them know they better stop if they wanted to get the rest of the way to town.

Once they got there, Parker's mother drove to the west side of the town square and parked in front of Johnson's Hardware. As she got out and shut her door, she looked through the window and said, "Now I'm going to be in here for a little bit, and then I'm going to go Mary Ann's dress shop. You boys go do whatever you want. Just be back here by 11:30 so we can have some lunch before we get the groceries."

"Do either of you have a watch?" she asked. When they shrugged their shoulders, she said, "That's okay. I'm not surprised. When I was your age I never had one either. Time didn't seem to matter. Anyway, just check the courthouse clock ever once in a while so you won't be late. I'll see you later."

She stepped up on the sidewalk and opened the door to the hardware store. The boys got out of the truck and walked across the street to a bench underneath an oak tree on the courthouse lawn so that they could plan their attack in the shade.

"So, what d'ya wanna do? It's your big day out," Parker said.

"Oh, I don't know. I'm just glad to be able to see some people. Why don't we over to the drugstore and get a Dr. Pepper."

"What d'ya think, any chance Lacey might be there, big guy?" Parker asked with a sly grin.

"I wouldn't have any idea. I just wanted to see if they had the new *Western Horseman*."

"Hey, don't worry. We just got the new one. I'll let you borrow it, and then we won't have to waste our time going over there," Parker offered.

"Thanks, buddy. But, let's go anyway just to stretch our legs."

As Parker got up from the bench, he looked over at Joe Dan and saw he was taking off his boots, but then pulling them back on again, this time with his pants legs stuck inside.

"Cowboy's in town, huh?" Parker said as he gave his friend a not-too-gentle shove in the direction of the drugstore.

When they got to the other side of the courthouse, they saw a dirty white pickup pull into a space across the street in front of Ragsdale Drugs. It was their friend, Jiggs, the esteemed former cow boss of the CS Ranch.

The old man opened the truck door and stiffly got out. As usual, he wore button up Levis with no belt and a white shirt buttoned at the collar. His black hat held a crease as only he could wear it. He had a pen and note book in the left pocket of his shirt and a can of Copenhagen in the right.

As he shut the door, he looked up and saw the boys walking toward him. He smiled at them and as they got close enough to shake hands, he asked with a grin, "How can you boys punch cows if you're walking around town?"

"Oh, we've been working so hard, we got the day off," Joe Dan laughed as he shook the man's hand.

"I bet you have. Parker, how's that colt?"

"He's doing good. He sure is good natured. Kinda like his mom," the boy replied.

"Well, I need to come out and see him. Say, you boys have been telling me forever that you were going to come to my camp so we could have a meeting. Now, when's that going to happen?" Jiggs asked.

"By gosh, we're gonna do it. How about this weekend? Maybe Saturday. We just gotta check with our folks," Joe Dan said.

"That'd be fine with me. But I want you to come hungry. I'm going fry you some chicken fried steak and make some gravy. You just let me know. Both your dad's have my phone number. Maybe we'd even have time for me to beat you in a few games of dominos."

"Okay, it's settled. We'll call you as soon as we know it's all right," Parker said as he shook Jiggs' hand again.

"All right, you boys just saddle those broncos of yours and lope over. I'll see you then. I gotta go right now and get my glasses fixed. I haven't hardly been able to see a thing since that colt of mine stepped on them."

He shook hands with the boys one more time and stepped up onto the sidewalk. He walked carefully with a slight limp, a condition he had gained honestly from over fifty years of riding bucking horses on the ranch. He was another of their heroes and easily the one they most revered. They liked how he joked with them, but at the same time talked to them like they were men. And they both recognized how much they learned from him. He knew more about cows, horses, and life than anybody they knew, and they loved to quiz him, especially about the old days when he was a kid punching cows for the CSs. Joe Dan once commented, "He doesn't even know he's teaching us."

After the boys watched him walk down the sidewalk, they went into the drugstore and took seats on stools in front of the lunch counter.

Mrs. Gunnerson stepped in front of them on the other side of the counter and said, "Well, how are you boys? I haven't seen you probably since the 4th of July. Your folks keep you working that hard?"

"Oh, probably not, but we've just been doing a lot of stuff," Joe Dan said. Before he had a chance to rattle off too much about their summer adventures, Parker interrupted and said, "Mrs. Gunnerson, before he gets too far into his stories, would you mind bringing us a couple of Dr. Peppers?"

"And a couple of moon pies, too," Joe Dan added.

"Coming right up," she said as she turned toward the drink machine.

After she delivered their drinks and moon pies, she excused herself and said she had to go back to the kitchen.

"I don't know how she's going to stand it not getting to listen to those good stories of yours," Parker said.

"Oh, you're just jealous because you ain't got much of a personality and even less to say," his friend replied as he took a long drink and then a bite of his pie.

"Yeah, I'm sure that's it. But anyway, we need to get it set tonight so that we can go see Jiggs," Parker said. "I can't wait to eat that chicken fried steak."

Talking about food reminded him about meeting his mother. He looked around at the big drugstore clock and saw that it was a little after eleven o'clock.

"Let's drink up, it's about time to go meet my mom," he said.

After they finished their snack, they paid Mrs. Gunnerson and walked out into the bright sunshine. Sure enough, the first person they saw on the sidewalk was Lacey Taylor and her best friend, Gabby. Both girls wore white halter tops and shorts and each had her hair pulled back into a pony tail, one blonde, the other, brunette.

"Hi," Parker said as he smiled at the girls. "What're you guys doing?"

"Oh, we thought we might go swimming this afternoon at the country club. You guys want to come with us?" said Lacey.

Parker noticed that Joe Dan hadn't come up even with him

to talk to the girls and how Lacey had to look over his shoulder even to see him.

"What do you think, Joe Dan? I don't think my mom would mind visiting Mrs. Dandridge for a while, while we took a dip."

"Oh, I don't know," Joe Dan said still holding back. "We don't have swimming suits and besides your mom said we had to get groceries."

"Don't worry, I can get some of my brother's suits," Gabby said. "Come on, it'll be fun. It's way too hot to not be in the water."

"Thanks anyway, but I guess we just better get on with our work," Joe Dan said as he walked past the girls without looking at them.

Parker exchanged puzzled looks with the girls and shrugged his shoulders. "I don't know what's wrong with him. I guess we'll just have to do it next time."

"Okay," Lacey said, "And when we do try to get your partner in a better mood."

"I'll see what I can do, but I'm not promising," as he said goodbye and started after Joe Dan.

When he caught up to him, he said, "Well, that was a first-class performance, Romeo. I thought I was the one that didn't know how to do around girls. I hope I'll be able to do as good as you my own self someday."

"Mind your own business and get in the truck," Joe Dan said.

They sat in silence a few minutes. Just as Parker was about to ask Joe Dan what his deal was with Lacey, his mother opened the door to the pickup.

"Well, Lordy be. I could have sworn I was going to have to go look for you two."

"We'll fool you every time, won't we?" Joe Dan said, glad he wasn't going to have answer any more of Parker's questions.

15

PLAYING CATCH

Aweek later Parker's dad called Jiggs on his cell phone.

"Are you sure you don't mind if those boys ride over to your camp? I'd hate for them to get in your way," he said.

"Oh, don't worry about it. I'm really not doing much, anyway. It's just a lot cooler up here in the summer than that darn bunkhouse at headquarters," Jiggs replied. Parker's dad knew that's what he would say, but he wanted to make sure that he accorded the man proper respect.

"All right then, I'll send 'em up Saturday morning."

When Parker's dad told him about the phone call, Parker immediately called Joe Dan. "Why don't you ride over Friday night so we can get an early start. Jiggs told my dad that we could spend the night."

"Good deal. But, how'll we get our beds to his camp?" Joe Dan asked.

"Dad said he'd have Andy drive 'em over a day or two before. Just have somebody bring yours over whenever they come this way."

"Okay, I'll see you Friday."

When Joe Dan rode in on Friday afternoon, the sight of him made Parker laugh to himself. He was dressed like Jiggs in a white shirt buttoned to the top and his Levis stuck into his boots. But he decided not to call him Little Jiggs, thinking there was no need to charge his buddy up especially in light of the Lacey incident.

After Joe Dan unsaddled and grained Centavo, he said, "What say we play catch for awhile."

"You bet, I've been missing the ol' ball glove ever since baseball's been over."

He walked into the saddle house and got his gloves and a ball. He gave the fielder's glove and ball to Joe Dan and then put on the catcher's mitt.

"You know, if I didn't like punchin' cows so much, I'd probably just go play in the major leagues," Parker said.

"Well, I bet you would. It's just that easy. Would you pick the team you wanted to play for or just wait for one of them to pick you?" his friend said as he grinned at him.

"Oh, I don't know. I'd probably wait and see who needed my rifle arm and faultless glove the most before I made any decision. All I know is that the Dodgers wouldn't get me. I'm still mad at them for beating the Rockies so many times."

"Well I bet you'd turn that situation around pretty quick, compadre, what with the skills you've got. But for now, let's just see if you can even still catch."

They played for about an hour until they heard Parker's mother calling from the back porch that supper was ready. After they washed their hands, they sat at the kitchen table anticipating eating the good spaghetti and garlic bread that Mrs. Smith had prepared.

"Where's dad?" Parker asked.

"He and Andy had to pull the windmill in the Martinez. I keep trying to get him to put in a solar pump over there, but like you know as well as I do, he's not going to try anything new and different. I'm surprised we even get him to use a cell phone."

"Yeah, it's like one side of his brain is in the 19th Century and the other's in the 21st," Parker said.

After the boys finished, they put their plates in the sink and went outside to play more catch. Josie was beside herself because Parker had been so intent on his throwing and catching that he forgot to throw some for her to retrieve which was, as far as she was concerned, the primary reason he was out there.

Finally, he noticed her and apologized. "I'm sorry. I wasn't paying attention," he said to her as he sailed the ball into the horse pasture for her. She dashed off in a cloud of dust, yelping as she went.

When she returned and dropped the ball at Parker's feet, he saw that she'd gotten it pretty slobbery. "Sister, I wish you didn't have to get them so wet. It makes 'em hard to throw."

Josie's expression showed that she could have cared less. Instead she pointed her ears at him and waited as patiently as she could to see where he would throw it next. This time, he threw it into the back of the feed truck. It took her a little time to smell out exactly where it was, but as soon as she did, she jumped in the back of the truck, grabbed it, and, obviously pleased with herself, bounced her way back to Parker.

"Boy, aren't you the smart one? I can never get anything past you," he said as he rubbed her neck. "Now go on, we need to finish before it gets dark."

They played for another fifteen minutes and then put the gloves up and went into the house to watch television.

16

JiGGS' CAMP

It was overcast when the boys got up the next morning and started to rain as the boys saddled their horses. The light rain felt good to the boys after the ninety degree heat they'd had over the last three weeks.

"I don't even think I'll put on my slicker," Joe Dan said.

"Yeah, me neither," Parker said. "I hate to ever have to put it on. It's so hot that sometimes I think it gets wetter on the inside of the thing than the outside. Besides, it seems like I always find some tree that tries to grab it and pull me off my horse."

It was fifteen miles to Jiggs' camp in Caliente Canyon and even at a buggy trot, it was going to take all morning to get there. By the time they got to the gate that led into the Caliente, the sky had cleared, the sun was shining, and their horses had broken a sweat.

"Gosh, wouldn't this be the life, to spend the summer up in country like this. Nothing to do but saddle a horse everyday and prowl cows. And no one to tell you to pick up your room or to do chores. We're going to have to do it as soon as they let us," Parker said.

"You bet. All we got to do is get Jiggs to show us how to make biscuits and fix chicken fried steak."

After they went through the gate, they hit a trot up the canyon and got to Jiggs' camp a little past noon. They tied their horses to the hitching rail in front of the two room cabin and walked up the steps. The front door was closed so they figured that Jiggs hadn't come back from prowling his cows. Each picked out a straight backed chair on the porch and sat down to wait for their friend.

When he hadn't shown up in thirty minutes, Joe Dan started to get antsy. He displayed his discomfort by first shuffling his feet, then alternately tapping the floor with one foot and then the other, and then standing up and walking to the end of the porch and back several times, all the while looking up and down the canyon in hopes of seeing Jiggs.

"Would you sit down," Parker said. "You're making me nervous."

"Well, I can't help it. I thought he'd be here by now."

"You're right. I can't hardly see how he would let his work get in the way of his visiting with us. We'll have to talk to him about it," his friend said with a grin.

"I tell you what. Why don't we find his dominos and practice a little bit before he gets here."

"Oh, I guess so, I'll go see if I can find them," Joe Dan said as he walked into the cabin.

The inside was dark but smelled of a mixture of wood smoke, horse sweat, and oats. Joe Dan let his eyes adjust and saw the wood cook stove on the west end flanked on each side by wooden shelves that held containers holding flour, baking powder, coffee, and pinto beans along with assorted canned goods.

There was a table in the middle with two chairs and a stool and a kerosene lamp on top. At the other end of the room in the corner was a rusty bed with Jiggs' bed tarp spread out on top. Next to the bed was a small table that held another lamp, a few coins, a pocketknife, and two cans of Copenhagen. Above the head of the bed was a shelf with some twenty books stacked in it. Joe Dan didn't want to take the time right then to find out what kind of stuff Jiggs read but promised himself to peruse the titles later.

On the wall beside the bed there was a framed print of a Frank Hoffman painting of two men relaxing on the side of a hill holding their horses by the reins and watching a herd of Hereford cattle in the valley below. Opposite the foot of the bed and in the corner next to the front door was a 55-gallon barrel that Joe Dan figured contained horse feed. There were several bridles, cinches, and latigos hung on nails above and beside it. One prominent nail was empty but was probably where the old man hung his leggings.

Joe Dan looked through the door that led to the other room of the cabin and saw several more metal bunks, two of them containing Parker's and his beds. There was a rock fireplace at the far end of the room with a Winchester 30.30 hung above the mantle.

He turned around and found the dominos stuck in among the canned goods by the side of the stove. He walked outside with them, and the boys moved their chairs on either side of a small wooden table that sat underneath one of the two windows that looked out from the front porch. Parker took the box from Joe Dan and emptied the dominos onto the table and the boys started putting them face down.

"You draw first for the down," Parker said after he shuffled the dominoes.

Joe Dan drew a seven, and Parker drew a four. "Hot dog," Joe Dan exclaimed. "I've just about got you beat already."

"Yeah, I guess that might be right if you only knew how to count," Parker countered.

They each drew seven dominos and Joe Dan played the double five. "Ten points," he said matter of factly.

Parker responded by playing the five-blank. "I think I'll take the same."

Joe Dan looked up at him from his dominos and said, "I'd rather be good than lucky."

Parker ignored his look and said, "I bet you would, big guy. Go ahead and play."

They had been playing for about fifteen minutes when they heard a dog bark down the canyon. They looked up and saw Jiggs jogging up through his horse trap riding a well-made bay horse with a star on his forehead and a left hind stocking. His dog, Corky, trotted by his side. The minute Josie saw him, she bounded off the porch and ran to him. They greeted each other with friendly canine sniffs and then followed Jiggs' horse up to the cabin.

"I see you boys didn't get lost trying to find me," the man said after he stepped off his horse. He dropped his reins to the ground knowing that the horse would stand and walked stiff legged up to the cabin steps.

When he got onto the porch he asked, "You boys been gamblin'?"

"No, not yet. This man's pretty tight with his money," Joe Dan said with a smile.

"Well, at least I have some," Parker replied as both boys stood to shake hands with the older man.

"Well, I'll try to see that both of you have a little bad luck after a while, but now I think we better have a little coffee and get something to eat."

He walked past the boys into the cabin and bent down and picked up three pieces of kindling from the box by the door. He put them in the fire box of the stove and then lifted the stove lid and poured kerosene from a jug over the wood. After he lit them with a kitchen match, he replaced the lid and filled the coffee pot with water from a bucket he kept on the right side of the stove.

"It won't take that too long to get going," he said to the boys who had followed him inside. "Could I interest you men in a little chicken fried steak?"

"You bet," Parker said. "It's our favorite."

"Mine too. I'll make us a few biscuits, too, so that we'll have something to sop up the gravy with. I tell you what. While that coffee's getting ready, let's go down and unsaddle our horses."

When they returned to the cabin, Jiggs took a can marked flour from the shelf by the stove plus a can of baking powder and walked to the table.

"Joe Dan, would you mind bringing over my grease from the stove and hand me that bowl sitting over there on the shelf by them cups?"

When Joe Dan brought them, Jiggs poured some flour into the bowl and added baking powder and salt from the shaker that sat on the table. After he'd stirred the mixture well with a fork, he used the fork to scoop out some bacon grease from the can and added it to the mixture.

"I hope you boys don't mind me using bacon grease, but it's about all I have. I know your mothers probably never use it. But, to me, biscuits ain't very good when they're made with shortening. I like 'em to have a little body to 'em," he said as he smiled at the boys.

"That's fine with us," Joe Dan said. "We like 'em any way you fix 'em."

After he'd cut in the grease with the fork, he poured in water from a pitcher that sat on the table and mixed everything together. When it was combined to the consistency he wanted, he forked it as a ball of dough out of the bowl onto the table and patted it down to three quarters of an inch with both hands.

"Joe Dan, would you get that ten-inch skillet hanging on the wall there and put it on the stove. And if you don't mind, Parker, put a few more pieces of wood in. We'll be having us some coffee before you know it."

He turned back to his dough and started cutting out biscuits with a jelly glass he had for the purpose. He handed the grease can to Joe Dan and said, "Put a little grease into that skillet so I can coat these biscuits. It'll make 'em taste better."

After he had the biscuits in the oven, the coffee pot had started to boil. He took off the lid and poured in coffee without measuring from a container that sat on the shelf. "I know you boys like you're coffee strong. Probably like you like your whiskey," he said with a mischievous grin.

The boys laughed. Joe Dan said, "You bet, the stronger the better as far as I'm concerned."

Next Jiggs took his knife from his pocket, opened it, and walked into the other room of the cabin. Joe Dan followed him and saw him slicing off a piece of meat from a steer carcass that hung from the ceiling beam. He laid the piece on Parker's bed tarp and started to cut another one. At one point he stopped his work and looked over at Joe Dan.

"His bed's clean, right?" he asked with another grin. "We wouldn't want to get any dirt in our food."

Joe Dan smiled back and said, "I think he washed it just last year."

"Good," the old man said and went back to his work. After he had cut six pieces from the carcass, he covered it with a piece of white canvas that seemed pretty dirty in its own right to Joe Dan.

Jiggs wiped his pocketknife on his pants, closed it, and returned it to his pocket. He picked up the meat and walked back to the cook stove. There he reached for a blue enameled bowl and put the meat inside and returned to the table and sat down.

"Parker, would you mind taking this bacon grease over to the stove and put about three spoons full into that skillet that hanging there on the right. And, if you don't mind go ahead and put some more wood in."

Parker did as he was asked. Jiggs poured some flour over the meat in the bowl and coated each piece with the flour. When he was satisfied each piece was coated well enough, he sat back in his chair and said to Joe Dan. "Son, I bet that coffee is just about ready. If you don't mind get a cup there from the wall and fill it with water and pour it in the pot to settle the grounds. We better have coffee before we go any further."

17

CHICKEN FRIED STEAK

The three sat at the table in front of their cups. Jiggs drank without letting his cool, while the boys waited until the black liquid wasn't quite so hot. "I could sure use some sugar," Joe Dan said to himself, "but I bet there isn't any for thirty miles."

After Jiggs finished his coffee, he stood up and said, "Well, boys, I better get this meat frying. I'd hate for you to get weak just because you haven't had anything to eat."

He took the bowl of floured meat to the stove and placed three pieces in the skillet with the hot grease. Soon the smell of the frying meat filled the room as it mixed with that of the biscuits in the oven.

When Jiggs judged the meat was done on one side, he took a fork and turned the three pieces over. Then he opened the oven door and peered inside.

"Better have another couple of minutes on those," he said.

He reached for a plate off of the shelf and forked the

meat from the skillet onto it. He replaced them with the last three pieces in the enamel bowl.

"Boys, I'm sorry I don't have any vegetables. Do you think you'll be able to get along without them?" he said with a grin.

"Oh, I guess so," Parker said smiling back.

After he turned the meat in the skillet, he opened the oven door. Satisfied the biscuits were done, he reached for a small towel that hung on a nail by the stove and used it to take the hot skillet and put it on top of the stove.

"Those don't look too bad. If they don't taste any good, maybe if you put a little gravy on 'em, they'll be better," he said.

Parker and Joe Dan looked at each other and grinned. "I'll bet we do all right with them," Parker said.

Jiggs then forked the meat from the skillet and gave the plate to Joe Dan to take to the table. He took a metal spoon with a wooden handle from the shelf and stirred the grease and drippings in the skillet. He added flour, salt, and pepper and then browned it. When he judged it was the right color, he poured water from the bucket and stirred the contents. As the mixture thickened, he added more water and pushed the skillet to the back where the stove was hottest.

When it started to bubble, he brought it back to the front, stirring as he did to make sure it didn't stick. He took the towel again and used it to carry the gravy to the table. Then he went back for the biscuits.

"Joe Dan, if you'd get us some plates and forks, I think we can eat," he said. "How about some more coffee?"

Both boys said they thought they'd had enough. "I'll just get us some water," Parker said as he walked over to fill their cups from the bucket.

"Suit yourself," Jiggs said, "but, if you don't mind, I think I'll take another jag."

Parker took the towel from him and brought the coffee pot over to fill his cup. After they were seated, all three pulled out their pocket knives, and Jiggs forked a piece of steak onto the plate of each boy and took one for himself.

"Now you boys don't be shy. I don't want to have to give any of it to the dogs."

"I don't think you'll have to worry," Joe Dan said as he broke open two biscuits and spooned gravy over them. "Please pass the pepper."

"Growing up, my dad always told me that if you eat a lot of pepper, you'll never get sick. And I guess I'm proof," Jiggs said.

The three ate in silence. After the boys finished a second piece of steak and two more biscuits, Jiggs asked, "There's still a couple of biscuits for you and quite a bit of gravy. What d'ya say?"

"No more for me. As much as I'd like to, I couldn't eat a drop more," Parker said.

"Yeah, I'm about to founder my own self," Joe Dan said.

"Well, okay. I just wanted to make sure you got enough. Now we better get these dishes washed so that we can play a game or two. Joe Dan, if you don't mind, take one of them plates and split open the rest of the biscuits and pour gravy over them for the doggies. Just set the plate outside on the porch so they can get to it."

Jiggs went to the stove and filled two dish pans with hot water from a large container that sat on the right side. After he poured in dish washing soap into one of them, he picked up the dish rag and turned to the boys and asked, "Who wants to wash?"

"I will," Joe Dan said. The boys worked quickly while Jiggs sat at the table, drank another cup of coffee, and smoked his pipe. When the boys were through, he had them pour the dish water outside on a fir tree that he'd transplanted next to the cabin.

When they returned, he had the dominos spread out on the table. "Which one of you wants to keep score?" he asked.

"Better let me. Joe Dan gets nervous anytime he has to deal with numbers over five," Parker said with a grin.

"Actually, that's about the truth. I'm not much of a mathematician," Joe Dan agreed.

Jiggs shuffled the dominos. "Okay, let's draw for the down."

Parker picked a domino and turned it over. "Four and three makes seven."

Joe Dan drew the one-four, and Jiggs drew the double ace. "Okay, Parker, it's yours," he said.

Parker drew seven dominos and, after studying them, played the double five. "Ten points," he said as he marked his score.

"I knew you had that one because it didn't take you very long to play it," Jiggs said with a grin.

"I'll take the same," Joe Dan said as he played the blank five.

"That hurt me," Jiggs said as he played the five two for no score.

As the game progressed, Joe Dan scored almost every time it was his turn and won the game handily. "For a man who says he's doesn't know math, you sure know how to count dominos," Jiggs said.

Try as he might, Joe Dan couldn't suppress a grin. "Let's play another one."

"Yeah, the winners always want to play again," Parker said as he poked his friend in the ribs.

Jiggs won the next game, and Parker the next. As they played, the boys periodically yawned feeling the effects of the good meal. When the last game was over, Jiggs said, "Well, boys, I think it's about time we hit the sack. What d'ya say." Both boys nodded in agreement.

"But, I tell you what. We can't leave this playing even. Let's draw high domino for the winner," Jiggs said.

The boys smiled at each other and Parker said, "That's okay with us."

Jiggs shuffled the dominos and said, "It's my camp, so I'll go last. Which one of you is oldest?"

"I'm older than he is by four months," Parker said.

"Well, okay. You draw first," Jiggs said.

Parker looked at the dominos and turned one over from the right side. "Six – three."

"All right, Joe Dan, let's see what you can do," Jiggs said.

Joe Dan leaned over the table and reached for a domino on the far side. "Four – five."

"Well, that's just about even," Jiggs said as he picked up one of the dominos closet to him. He looked at it knowingly, smiled at the boys, and said, "Sorry, you men had bad luck," as he turned over the double five. "But remember, whether you win or lose, it's still pretty cheap entertainment."

"Ah, shoot. We'll get you the next time," Parker said as he stood and shook the old man's hand.

"That'd be good. I like playing with you guys because you don't take forever. Now, go ahead and roll out your beds. We're going to be up early and I'm going to get some more biscuits and gravy in you before you ride home."

18

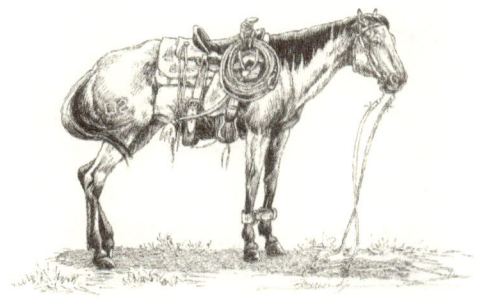

LOOKING FOR RELICS

Two weeks before school was to start in the fall Parker and Joe Dan made plans to explore Templeton Canyon, a long, deep canyon on the west side of Joe Dan's ranch. Many people had told them that Indians had once lived there, and even though they'd been in the canyon before on picnics with their parents, they'd never had time to explore it. Now that they were old enough to go by themselves, they were feeling like Indiana Jones and were looking for adventure.

On Friday morning Parker caught Chester after breakfast. When he had him fed and saddled, he mounted and rode to the back gate of the house and called to his mother.

After a bit she opened the screen door, smiled at him, and said, "You boys be careful and have a good time."

Parker said, "Oh, Mom, you don't need to worry. We can take care of ourselves."

"I know you can, but be careful anyway," she replied as she waved goodbye.

The boy waved back and reined toward the trail that

led to Joe Dan's ranch. Josie fell in behind. Once Parker had gone through the horse trap gate and shut it, he hit a buggy trot through the piñons and junipers that dotted the west side of Ortega Mesa where the trail led.

It took more than an hour to cross the ridge that overlooked the Bar P Ranch. Parker had always liked the headquarters of Joe Dan's ranch. Every building was painted white with red trim and had a red shingle roof. The ranch yards were neat and free of clutter and were shaded by giant cottonwood trees that kept the place cool even during the hottest days of summer.

Parker dropped off the ridge and rode for the corrals nestled under the trees by the creek that ran south of the ranch. He knew Joe Dan would be waiting.

Sure enough he was. He saw him standing in front of the saddle house holding Centavo by the rein. They waved to each other, and Joe Dan led his horse out of the big corral, shut the gate, and stepped on.

"I sure hope we find something," Joe Dan said.

"I do to," said Parker. "At least some arrowheads or hatchets or something."

They pointed their horses to the trail that led to Templeton Canyon. It went almost straight up the side of the mesa on the west side of the ranch, but once they got on top, it flattened out, and they rode through several stands of ponderosa pine that were interspersed through the open parks. The sun was warm on their backs as they rode along and talked. Being that they hadn't seen each other for two weeks, they had a lot to catch up on and, as usual, Joe Dan took the lead and worked hard to tell everything he needed to before they got to their destination.

"Did you hear that John Mason broke his leg when he was chasing his sister last Tuesday?" he asked.

"No, I didn't," Parker replied. Before he had a chance to ask a question, Joe Dan continued, "I guess his mom was so mad at him for breaking his leg and making her take him to the hospital that she grounded him from playing football."

Parker laughed. "Well, won't it be kinda hard for him to play football with a broken leg anyway?"

"Yeah, I know what you're saying. But you know how parents get when they get mad at you."

They rode to the end of the mesa and dropped off on a game trail that they discovered underneath two ponderosa pines. It was steep, but the horses easily slid down it on their hind legs and before long the boys were at the bottom of the canyon.

Templeton Canyon stretched several miles to the west and even though it's was fairly wide where they entered, it narrowed quickly toward its head with steep perpendicular cliffs on both sides. It was noon when the boys rode up to the little creek that ran down the middle of the canyon and stopped to water their horses.

Joe Dan fished out two packages of beef jerky from his saddle pockets and threw one to Parker. They chewed on the jerky while their horses rested and then they got back on and headed up the canyon. They rode along, looking up at both sides of the canyon and after a while, Parker noticed an overhang on the south side that had black smudge marks near the top.

"Look up there," he said as he pointed to the spot. "It sure looks like there could have been a fire sometime under that overhang. What do you think?"

"Well, we won't know unless we look," said his friend, and they pointed their horses to the foot of the canyon wall.

They tied their horses' reins to an oak tree and started climbing toward the overhang. The climb was steep and made more difficult because of the loose rocks that covered the lower part of the cliff. But they steadily made their way up, only sometimes losing their footing. When they got to the bottom of the overhang, they discovered a juniper tree on the right side that looked like they could use to pull themselves up into the cave.

Parker took the lead and pulled himself onto the ledge. When he got to his feet, he looked up and shouted, "Bingo. You gotta see this."

In the shallow cave that spread out underneath the overhang, he saw a wall built out of rocks at the back and on each side of it two depressions that had rocks stacked around them.

As he took a step, he looked down and saw a three-inch arrowhead at his feet. "Holy cow," he cried. "I found one."

Joe Dan was just then climbing up by the juniper tree. He said, "Would you just go ahead and wait for me. I want to find something too."

"Don't worry, amigo. I think we've found us a jackpot," his friend replied.

They walked toward the rock wall lowering their heads as they went because the top of the cave sloped downward the farther they went. Three or four grinding stones were scattered on the floor of the cave, but not much else.

Joe Dan was getting anxious because he hadn't found something right away, but then he looked down to his left and saw the tip of an arrowhead embedded in the hard clay of the floor. Dropping to his knees, he pulled out his pocket knife and started digging. He soon uncovered a shiny grey point that was almost as long as his hand. Standing up, he rubbed off the dirt and saw that part of the base of the point had broken off.

"Hey, what about this," he said as he handed it to Parker.

"It's a beauty. As big as it is, it was probably a spear point, don't you think?" Parker said.

"Well, let's see what's behind that wall, ya want to?" Joe Dan said.

"Sure. Might as well since we're here," Parker replied.

Even though it was dark in the back of the cave, they stepped forward, bending over more and more as they went. Joe Dan grabbed the top of the wall and started to swing his right leg over, but before his foot touched the floor on the other side both boys heard a rattling and swishing that they knew meant nothing more than a snake.

"Son of a gun. What's he doing in there?" Parker said.

"I don't know, and I don't want to find out," replied Joe Dan as he ran back to the front of the cave. Wide-eyed, he started inspecting the floor of the cave in case there might be anymore unwelcome residents around. "Ya never can find a stick around when you need one, can you?" he said as he backed even closer to the edge of the cave.

"No, you sure can't. I don't know about you, but all of a sudden I'm not that interested in whatever's behind that wall. I bet it's nothing good, anyway," Parker said.

"I'm with you," said Joe Dan and they both started toward the juniper tree so they could climb down.

As Parker almost reached the tree, he looked past it to the wall of the cave. He hadn't noticed when they first climbed up, but now he saw that the wall had all kinds of pictures and signs pecked into it where it had been smudged black by the smoke of the Indians' fires. Mostly the pictures were circles and squiggly lines, but there were also several hand prints and a horse and what looked like an insect playing a musical instrument.

The boys walked closer to the wall carefully stepping over sticks and rocks that scattered the ground. They traced their fingers over the pictures and marks and then stepped back to get a better view of them.

"I wonder what they mean, and who made 'em? Joe Dan asked.

"Beats me," Parker replied. "Makes you wonder if some old Indian was really trying to draw something important or if he was just doodlin'?"

Suddenly, a gust of wind swept through the cave, swirling dirt and leaves around the boys. They both looked wide-eyed at each other, gripped with a feeling that made the hair stand up on the back of their necks.

"Well, I don't know about you, but I think somebody doesn't like us asking questions," Parker said. "Let's get out of here."

"I'm with you," replied Joe Dan, and they started for the tree. "Maybe that's why that snake lives here," he said as he dropped off the ledge.

Before long they were back to where their horses were tied. Parker walked up to Chester, and the moment he reached for the bridle rein to untie him, another gust of wind came up the canyon. Chester snorted and pulled back on the reins with his eyes wide like he'd just seen something he didn't like. Before Parker could catch him to settle him down, he broke the rein and trotted off about thirty feet down the canyon where he stopped and started shaking.

"What in the world's wrong with you," Parker yelled as he started after him.

Although Centavo stamped his feet and also seemed unsettled, Joe Dan got on him okay and rode past Parker and grabbed Chester's rein before he could go any further.

"Now that's weird. Chester's never done that before," Parker said as he used his pocket knife and a leather string from his chaps pocket to repair the broken rein. Once he had it mended, he mounted. Joe Dan looked at him with wide eyes. "I know what you mean. I think we better quit asking questions and just get out of here.

They spurred their horses into a run and didn't stop until they got to the mouth of the canyon. There, they slowed to a walk, but Parker could tell Joe Dan wasn't comfortable with the pace. "We can't run these horses all the way home, you know," he said.

"I know," Joe Dan said, "but this place gives me the heebie-jeebies, and I ain't scared of nothing."

"Yeah, right, cowboy. I've heard that before," Parker replied. "But I bet there isn't much more up there anyway, and even if there is, I think we ought to leave it for somebody else to find."

They turned in to the trail and didn't say anything or look back until they came to Joe Dan's outside fence. After Parker closed the gate behind them and got back on his horse, he said, "Whatever's up there, I think we ought to just let them have it. Next time we'll go over to Ortega Mesa because I know nobody will spook our horses over there. You know what I mean?"

"You ain't gonna get a fight out of me," Joe Dan said as he turned his horse toward home.

LABOR DAY GATHER

Parker dropped off the south side of Manuelas Canyon behind seven pairs of cows and calves. When the cattle reached the bottom, they trotted to the creek and watered. It was a cool and cloudy day, unusual for a Labor Day weekend in northern New Mexico.

Parker thought earlier in the day that the weather would probably mess up a lot of people's holiday plans. On the other hand, it would have no effect on his weekend because it was the time every year his dad started the fall gather of the Box S cows and calves. And importantly, it was the last weekend of the summer before school started, so Parker and Joe Dan were available to help. "Besides," Parker said to himself, "I'd rather be horseback gathering cows in the mountains than going on a picnic anyway."

On the other side of the canyon, but farther up, Joe Dan and Andy were slowly driving a bunch they had gathered and that would soon rendezvous with Parker's cattle.

"Have you watched any football games yet?" Andy asked Joe Dan.

"Naw. I'm still watching as many baseball games as I can. I can't believe that the playoffs and then the World Series are just another month off."

"Yeah, me too. I hope the Rockies get in it."

"I think they will if their pitching holds up."

When their cattle met Parker's, they rode past them to a sun lit vega where Parker was sitting on the ground next to his horse. "How many did you get?" Andy asked.

"Seven pair here, but another thirty-three that I kicked down to the gate."

"Boy, that's good. From all that we gathered, I calculate we ought to have more than half of 'em. I wonder how your Dad and John are doing? The last time I saw them they had a pretty big bunch and were coming off that bench above the falls."

"Yeah, I hope they're doing good, but I'm more interested in what your mom's going to bring us for dinner," Joe Dan said to Parker.

"Me too. That four o'clock breakfast seems like a long time ago."

It was warm in the sunshine. Andy and Joe Dan took off their Levi jackets and tied them behind the cantles of their saddles. They continued to talk but soon heard cattle moving through the trees by the creek up the canyon.

"Well, boys, we better go see if we can help 'em," Andy said.

Parker got back on Chester, and the three trotted toward the cattle. When they met up with them, they veered to the left to be out of the way of the leaders and soon met Tom Smith and John Robles driving them from behind.

"How did you men do?" Tom asked.

"Pretty good. My count says we got one hundred and eighty-eight pairs," Andy said.

"Well, good. There's over a hundred in this bunch, and we heard James coming behind us with hopefully the rest of them. Why don't we just ease everything down to the mouth of the canyon so they can pair up. Then we can see what Ann brought for us for dinner."

The five riders took places behind the cows and calves that had stopped to drink from the creek. Andy crossed the creek and pulled alongside the lead cattle to start them moving down canyon. Parker did the same on the other side.

"Well, Tom, your calves sure did well in here this summer. They're as nice a set of calves as I've seen in a long time," said John.

"Yeah, I'm really proud of them. Now, if the market will just hold, we ought to do pretty well this year."

The mouth of the canyon was about four miles away, but the cattle moved easily as if they understood that summer was drawing to a close, and that it was time to go to winter pasture. As the cowboys turned a bend in the canyon, Parker looked up when he caught a whiff of smoke from a fire. He rode to the top of a low hill and saw his mother about a half mile away tending a cooking fire.

The riders dropped the cattle a quarter of a mile past where Ann Smith had set up her cooking fire. They turned back toward her, and when she saw them, she called out, "Well, hi there. Any of you hungry?"

"You can bet I am," Joe Dan was first to say.

"Well, get down. I think it's about ready."

The cowboys hobbled their horses away from the fire and walked to the creek to wash their hands. Tom Smith and John Robles came back first, and Tom walked up to his wife and kissed her. "Thanks for doing this for us, honey" he said.

"Oh, you know I like to do it. Besides, I don't like to see my boys hungry when they've been working hard."

Joe Dan walked up and hugged her. "Boy, am I hungry."

He looked at all of the skillets and Dutch ovens on the cook fire and said, "I bet you made those fried potatoes just for me, didn't you."

"Well, of course I did. I know they're your favorite. But I also knew you wouldn't mind having a little brisket and some pinto beans to go with them either. Now go get a plate and load up," she said.

The older men filled metal cups with coffee from the pot that hung from the fire and squatted on their boot heels next to the fire, while the boys retrieved plates and silverware from the chuck box. One by one they passed by the fire and filled their plates as high as they could. The last Dutch oven was full of golden brown biscuits.

Parker fished out two of them when he went past and said, "Mom, I don't even think I'm going to need any butter for these."

"Well, that's good, because I didn't bring any. I thought you boys could probably get along without it." And then she said, "Oh, I almost forgot."

She left the fire and stepped to the side of the pickup to bring out a large plastic tub with a lid on it. "I've got salad for you too. I knew you all wouldn't like it if you didn't have something green along with the rest of it," she said.

"You're exactly right," Joe Dan said with a grin. "I never mind salad as long as there's enough dressing on it."

Ann Smith smiled back at him and shook her head, "You boys."

Tom stood up and walked over to her. "Honey, let me get you a plate so you can sit down and rest."

"Why, thank you. How kind of you," she said as she hugged his neck.

Everyone sat cross legged underneath a tall cottonwood tree with their plates in their laps. At first there was little conversation among them but soon they slowed their eating and starting talking about the morning's gather and events that were coming up in the fall.

"Parker, how's that colt coming along?" John asked.

"Just fine. He's growing right along. I'm just about to finish getting him halter broke so that we can wean him."

"Well, I know you'll have a good time starting him when he comes two. And, by the way, I'm going to have a couple of colts that I'd like you and Joe Dan to start next summer if you would."

Parker and Joe Dan looked at each other and smiled. "You bet," Joe Dan said. "We've just been waiting for the chance."

When everyone finished eating, they took their plates to a pan Ann had set out on the back of the pickup. "Mom, we'll get these dishes when we get home," Parker said.

"Oh, that's sweet of you son, but you guys go ahead and take care of your cattle. It won't take me long to clean up when I get back."

"All right boys." Tom said. "Go catch your horses. We better get these cows started for the XL before it gets too far along in the afternoon. You boys start 'em, and John and I'll count 'em out through the gate.

When the cows and calves were through the gate, Tom Smith got off his horse and closed it. "Well, it looks like we missed four pair," he said to the mounted riders who had stopped and turned toward him.

"Wouldn't it be good if we could gather the remnants first?" John said with a laugh.

"Someday we need to figure out how to do that very thing," Tom smiled in return. He had been waiting for someone to come up with the old joke. Somebody always did.

As the riders fell in behind the cattle, a rush of cool wind came down the canyon. "Whew, I'm not quite ready for any kind of cold weather just yet. I was still wanting a little more summer," Joe Dan said as he pulled on his jacket.

"Well, amigo, it's all right with me," Parker said. "Whether you believe it or not, I'm actually looking forward to getting back to school."

He turned in his saddle and looked at the mountains they had just come from. They rose up massive and green. Soon, they would be covered in snow, but it didn't matter to him because he liked all of the seasons.

"You know partner, we've had a pretty good summer, haven't we?"

GLOSSARY

cantle: raised back of saddle seat

cattle guard: frame of metal bars or rails sunk at a gate opening that discourages cattle from crossing but allows vehicles to drive through

cowy: instinct in a horse to work cattle

crow hopping: stiff legged jumps by a bucking horse

dun: tan color with black legs, mane, and tail with often a dark stripe down the back

flankers: cowboys who throw calf on its side and hold it after roper has drug it to the branding fire

hobbles (ed): leather or rope restraints wrapped around horse's front legs to keep him from straying

horse colt: a male

horse trap: large fenced enclosure next to main corrals where saddle horses are pastured when not in use

jackpot: wreck or accident

mesa: flat topped mountain

outfit: general term for a ranch, its employees, and operation

pigging string: narrow diameter rope 3 to 4 feet in length used to tie calf's legs

prowl: to ride through cattle on horseback to check for sick or injured animals

quirt (quirtin'): short whip braided of rawhide or latigo leather used to encourage horse to greater speed

rigging: slang term for saddle

rowel: wheel of a spur

skirts: sheepskin lined leather pieces in back of saddle that rests on horse's back

slicker: cowboy's raincoat, usually yellow in color

swells: projections in front of saddle seat below saddle horn

trap: roper's loop thrown to ensnare animal's hind feet

twine: slang term for rope

vega: Spanish, hay or grass covered meadow

wood: slang term for saddle, named because a saddle is built on wooden foundation called a tree